MASTER OF THE CHASE

Susan Macias

A KISMET® Romance

METEOR PUBLISHING CORPORATION
Bensalem, Pennsylvania

To Denise, whose gorgeous red hair
and clever wit inspired the character
of Lauren. You have enriched my life
in ways you cannot imagine. My thanks
for the encouragement, friendship, and
support. Here's to the future. May it
be filled with all things good.

SUSAN MACIAS

Susan Macias has always read romances. In the
eighth grade, she got in trouble for hiding one behind
her algebra book in class. She gave up a promising
career in accounting to try her hand at writing and
has never looked back. Susan lives in Southern California with her husband. This prolific author loves to
hear from readers. You may write her directly at:
P.O. Box 801913, Santa Clarita, CA 91380-1913.

Other books by Susan Macias:

ONE

"The offer is generous, gentlemen," Jack Baldwin said as he leaned back in his chair. "And it *is* final."

He uttered the statement with conviction, then tossed his pen on the long, polished table. There was no sound in the room—no secretary taking notes, no distracting hum of air conditioning or half-heard office noises. The large executive boardroom was soundproof. With its rich leather chairs and fine wood furniture, it reeked of power and foreign money. Jack planned on leaving with his share of both.

The next few minutes would tell if he'd been successful. He watched with calm detachment as the seven executives of the Bolasieur Company leaned toward one another and spoke intently. Patience was the key. These men were not the enemy; they were the object of the hunt.

Murmured conversation drifted across the teak conference table. He listened with half an ear. The English was too faint for him to hear, and the French, well, they could shout it in his face and it wouldn't matter a damn. Despite two years of high school French and another year in college, the language eluded him. He could sniff out a deal at a hundred miles and see an opponent's weakness blindfolded, but foreign languages remained just that—foreign. It was a flaw, he admitted, pushing back his chair and rising to his feet. His secretary said it kept him human.

He walked slowly to the wide window taking up the better part of the north wall. Manhattan stretched out before him. He liked the city, enjoyed its energy and constant movement, but he didn't eat, sleep, and breathe it like the locals. When the meeting was over, he'd be glad to go home.

Behind him, the voices grew louder, more intense. The meeting would have been simpler with his translator. But Ned had been called home when his wife had gone into premature labor with their first child. It didn't matter. Jack preferred to work alone. They—those unnamed faces who started rumors and exaggerated reputations—called him a maverick and a gunslinger. Both descriptions pleased him.

There was a moment of silence, then the discussion continued behind him. He checked his watch. If they'd come to a decision, he would be able to make the eleven-o'clock flight back to Chicago. With the one-hour time difference, he could be at the Language Institute by two. With the victory, or defeat, of the French contract out of his hands, he found his attention wandering to the next prize. This time he was setting his sights on the East and Japan.

He smiled as he remembered his staff report saying Lauren Reese wasn't interested in joining the team. He'd never met the lady, but rumor had it she was the best. One way or the other, he'd convince her. He didn't believe in taking no for an answer. It was, he acknowledged, the key to his success.

"Monsieur Baldwin, we have made a decision."

Jack turned slowly, careful to keep his posture relaxed, his arms loose at his sides. Seven pairs of eyes studied him. The tension in the room mounted. Months of preliminary negotiations, hundreds of man-hours, thousands of international faxes and phone calls, all came down to this one moment.

He permitted himself a small smile. If the year were 1870, he'd be holding up a bank, or risking his stake on a pair of twos. No such luck. It was the nineties, and his bluff was for a multimillion-dollar contract. He'd have the French on his terms or he wouldn't have them at all. Hell of a way to make a living.

He walked over to the desk and leaned forward, his hands braced on the sleek wood. "Do we have a deal?"

The gray-haired man of the group rose from his chair at the far end of the boardroom and stepped up to Jack. "You don't, to quote your countrymen, believe in taking prisoners, do you, Monsieur Baldwin?"

"I wouldn't know what to do with them."

The Frenchman smiled suddenly and stuck out his manicured hand. "We have a deal."

Lauren Reese glanced down at the class of second graders sitting at her feet. Round eyes widened as she went on with her story.

"It got so cold that ice formed on the river, but still the Snow Monkey sat there, with his tail in the water."

"Wasn't he hungry?" a little blond girl asked.

"Yes. But the bear had told him to wait until he could feel the little fishes holding on. And as the ice grew thicker, he thought it was the fish. He was very pleased, thinking he was going to have a big meal all to himself.''

She reached for another large piece of cardboard that contained the next illustration to the story. It showed the Snow Monkey shivering on a log in the middle of a river.

''Then, when he decided he surely had enough fishes, he tried to pull his tail free of the ice. But he couldn't.'' She frowned in mock concern. ''No matter how hard he pulled and pulled, nothing happened.''

''He's stuck!'' a boy said, grinning at her. ''My baby brother got his head stuck like that in our stair railing. Mom had to call the fire department to get him out.''

''Did not,'' his friend said.

''Did, too!''

They began pushing each other. Their teacher moved from her place on the side of the room. ''Scott, Brian. Stop it, you two.''

Lauren smiled at the woman and shook her head. ''It's okay,'' she said, pulling a large whistle out of her pocket. ''I grew up with brothers.''

She blew it once, the high, piercing noise splitting the air. Instantly there was silence. Brian and Scott glared at each other one last time and returned their attention to her.

''Grabbing a branch high above him, the Snow Monkey held on really tight—'' she picked up the next picture ''—and . . .''

She scanned the room, noting the children's rapt gazes. There was a flash of movement by the back door, and she realized that someone had come in during her story.

Except for the lights on the small stage where she

sat, the room was dim. The tall, broad outline was obviously a man but didn't look like anyone she knew. Certainly not a staff member or administrator of the Language Institute. There was something powerful about the way he stood in the shadow, his long legs braced wide apart, his arms folded across his chest. He reminded her of a warrior guarding a treasure.

Their eyes met. There was no way to see features or to even be sure he was looking at her, but she sensed the connection. The pull, stronger than her resistance, made her think about running—toward him, toward the danger. About—

"Miss Reese." A girl tugged on her jacket sleeve. "What about the Snow Monkey?"

"What? Oh!" Lauren glanced down at the children all staring at her, then at the illustration in her hands. "He grabbed the branch and pulled with all his might. Finally there was a loud snap and he was free." She reached for the last picture. "But as you can see, he lost his tail."

The children gasped.

"Won't it grow back?"

"No. It's gone forever. And you see how red his face is?"

They nodded.

"Some people say it's because he pulled so hard trying to escape. But I think he's embarrassed about being greedy and wanting all those fish for himself."

Their teacher walked to the front of the room. "Why don't we give Ms. Reese a big round of applause for that great story."

The children clapped and called out their thank-yous.

"You're welcome," Lauren said, not daring to look toward the back of the room. What if the man was still there? "Mrs. Bryant is going to take you down the hall and show you a real tea ceremony."

"Yuk! I don't like tea." Either Scott or Brian, Lauren wasn't sure who was who, made a face.

She laughed. "Don't worry. You don't have to *drink* the tea. In fact, Mrs. Bryant has milk and cookies waiting for everyone."

The children rose and moved toward the door. A quick glance to the back of the room showed that the man no longer stood in the shadows. Before she could decide if she was disappointed or grateful, the tiny blond girl from the front row approached her.

"Do you think it hurt the monkey?" she asked, her blue eyes filling with tears. "Losing his tail like that?"

"No, honey. It's just a story." Lauren crouched down and took the small hands in her own. "A fable to explain something we don't understand. A lot of larger primates, like gorillas and chimps, don't have tails either. I promise, it doesn't hurt them."

The girl smiled. "Okay. I'm gonna go watch them pour tea. Thanks. 'Bye." She ran from the room.

Lauren rose to her feet and reached for the pile of illustrations. The overhead lights clicked on suddenly. She blinked and spun to see who was still in the room.

It was him.

"Good afternoon," she said. "May I help you?"

He walked forward until he stood directly in front of her. Even standing on the platform, she was slightly below his eye level. In an instant she recognized the handsome face, strong jaw, and stubborn chin. So he'd come after all.

They'd warned her he wouldn't give up without a fight. At the time, she'd thought their insistence exaggerated. Nothing could be that important. But now, facing him in person, she felt a flutter of gladness that they'd been right.

The color photographs in a local magazine hadn't lied about the deep black of his hair or the intriguing blue-gray eyes, but nothing had prepared her for the sheer power of his personality. It radiated out like a heat wave, melting her reserve, making her wonder if she'd been a little too hasty in her decision.

"I liked the way you told the story," he said. His low voice, strong yet seductive, caressed each word. The simple sentence spoke volumes as his gaze swiftly caressed her face, dipping slightly, then returning to hold her captive. "I didn't know the Language Institute had classes for children."

"We don't take them as students," she said, unable to turn away. "The Institute has adopted the local elementary school. The staff helps out in any way they can. Their teacher called and asked if we had anything about Japan for her second grade class. It's International Week at the school."

"You've done this before." He nodded toward the illustrations.

"It's one of my favorite stories."

"Interesting." He thrust his hands into his trouser pockets. "Why?"

"It's short, which helps with younger children, but there's a real message. And it's fun to tell stories about why animals look certain ways."

"So what's your explanation for the aardvark?"

"Low blood sugar?"

He grinned. The flash of white teeth and a dimple on his right cheek made him look less predatory, but only for a second. She knew what he wanted.

She walked to the edge of the stage and stepped

down. He took her arm for a moment, a brief, courteous gesture that meant nothing at all. Except she could feel the imprint of each finger long after he'd released her.

Now that they stood on the same level, her head barely came to his chin. At five five and wearing heels, she was usually considered on the tall side.

"Any chance of my watching the tea ceremony?" he asked.

"Why would you want to?"

"I've never seen one before. I'm interested in all aspects of Japanese culture."

"I'm surprised."

"Why?"

She shrugged. "You don't seem like the tea ceremony type."

His low chuckle made her lips curl up involuntarily. Danger signs flashed so brightly, she wondered why he didn't have to shield his eyes.

"Was that a yes or a no?" he asked.

Lauren stared at the fabric of his suit. The light gray wool looked soft enough to wear against bare skin. Expert tailoring and designer lines enhanced the breadth of his shoulders and chest. The red tie, the only splash of color on an otherwise conservative suit, spoke of power, success, and confidence.

"You strike me as a very Western man. The ceremony can be tedious for those who don't understand its simplicity and beauty."

The blue faded from his eyes, leaving behind an ever-darkening gray. Something flickered there, something hot but unreadable.

"You misjudge me," he said, his gaze never releasing her. "I know how to appreciate beautiful things."

She felt a blush stain her cheeks. He hadn't even hinted that he meant anything other than the ceremony, but for some reason, she knew he'd been saying more. Did he know? she wondered. Did he know she knew? Were they both playing a game, speaking of one thing but meaning another? He unsettled her with his deep voice and polished manners. She'd known he would. That's why she'd turned down the offer in the first place.

Oh, she knew all about Mr. Jack Baldwin. She knew what he wanted and why he was here, but there was no way *she* was going to be the one to mention it. It was his game; let him make the first move.

"How did you happen to hear about the Institute?" she asked as though he were any potential client.

"My staff."

Impressive, she thought. The complete truth and yet not the truth at all. He didn't care about the Institute. She was the reason he was here.

"How long have you been interested in Japan?"

He grinned. "Since I was old enough to read the financial pages. You can't play in the international market these days without being aware of their impact on every aspect of business."

"Understanding their stock market is very different from understanding their culture."

Again those mysterious eyes flashed with gray fire. "That's why I'm here. I want to understand everything." *And to own it*, was the unspoken part of his statement. Despite the business suit and clean-shaven features, he was as untamed as the wolf his reputation claimed him to be.

"Very well. The tea ceremony is just down the hall.

We can stand in the back, if you'd like. I don't want to distract the children."

"Certainly not."

He paused, as if waiting for her to lead the way. After all she'd read and been told, she'd been expecting to be persuaded. The man hadn't earned his reputation as one of the country's most determined and successful businessmen by giving up easily. But she'd never thought he'd approach her here—invade her workplace and then pretend he didn't know she knew.

Lauren swallowed hard, fighting the awkwardness that swept over her. When she took a step, she felt the light pressure of his hand resting on the small of her back. For the second time in as many minutes, he touched her. Again, the gesture could easily be dismissed as polite, even meaningless. But through the layers—her rust-colored linen suit jacket and skirt, the silk blouse and panty hose—she felt each long, masculine finger. His palm burned hotter, as if a brand were slowly being applied to her sensitized skin. She walked quickly, hoping to dislodge him, but he kept up easily.

"The room is, ah, through here."

She'd almost said his name aloud.

They walked down the hall, past two classrooms in session, then she opened a closed door and motioned for him to follow her. Once they were inside, she took a tiny half step away. The burning on the small of her back was replaced by a cool, bereft feeling she didn't dare analyze.

The class of second graders sat on the floor staring raptly at the stage. Two Japanese women, in formal dress complete with heavy black wigs and kimonos, performed the tea ceremony. Faint music drifted through the room; the high-pitched flute and strings added to the ambiance.

"The tea ceremony has a distinct order consisting of thirty-seven steps," she said softly, unwilling to disturb the tranquil atmosphere.

He glanced at her and raised dark eyebrows. "I'm not sure your young audience will appreciate the subtlety."

"We give them the short-attention-span treatment. It lasts about twelve minutes."

"I'd prefer the long version. There is something to be said for slowly capturing each nuance, savoring the differences . . . in culture, of course."

"Of course," she murmured.

Lauren had always considered herself an auditory person, but there was something unique about his voice that did more than spark her imagination. Each word fell from his lips, the fully formed vowels and consonants lingering in her mind long after the sound had faded.

They stood next to each other. Not close enough for her to feel the heat of his body or even inhale his scent, but that didn't make her any less aware.

She'd dealt with powerful men before. Even handsome ones. In the past, she'd been attracted, sometimes intrigued. There had been times, after the completion of a project, she dated a former client. But she'd never experienced this steady pull, as though an invisible line had hooked some inner part of her psyche and was slowly reeling her in. Jack Baldwin pursuing her might be a feather in her cap, career-wise, but personally, it could spell disaster. She'd been right to turn his people down.

"They'll be done in a minute," she said brightly

"Perhaps you'd like to make an appointment to speak with the director."

"Why?"

"You said you were interested in Japanese culture. We have several excellent classes, everything from history to language studies. Is this for you or will there be other company employees participating?"

The music stopped and the two women in the front of the room bowed. The children clapped, then rose and rushed toward the table set up with milk and cookies. Conversation exploded as nineteen seven-year-olds all began to talk at the same time.

Lauren shook her head. "I can see it would be futile to continue our conversation here. Let's go to my office."

Jack followed her from the room. The lines of her suit flowed loosely over her body, only hinting at the feminine curves below. He watched her hips sway provocatively with each step, beckoning him with an ancient and heady rhythm. His gaze climbed higher to the deep mahogany hair curling over her shoulders and back. He'd never cared for redheads, preferring the cool elegance of brunettes or the stop-dead-in-your-tracks beauty of sloe-eyed blondes. Lauren Reese might be a lot of things, but she wasn't obvious.

He searched for the right word to describe her, but it eluded him. Until now, he hadn't given her much thought, not as a person anyway. She filled his requirements. She was the best, and the key to his success with the Japanese company—therefore, he wanted her. End of story. Looks or personality played no part in the decision at all. He only cared about getting the job done, or in this case, the contract signed.

Now, seeing her, hearing her voice, watching her

handle herself with the children, he believed her reputation to be accurate, although he didn't have a clue as to what combination of qualities had convinced him. No matter the price, he would have her. On his terms. Just like the French.

She turned a corner, then motioned for him to enter the first door on his right. The office was large, a square space with a big window opening onto an inner courtyard. The mild April weather had melted the last of the snow, exposing tender grass and trees heavy with brave spring buds.

A carved desk, dark and ornate, dominated the room. Several watercolors graced the walls. The muted paints in one showed a single flower. Another depicted a pond. In the corner, a four-foot tree, carefully trimmed into steps of green needles and gray-brown bark, stood in a black lacquered pot. There weren't any framed and displayed degrees, no modern sculpture, no calculated photographs of her with successful and happy clients.

"It's not what I expected," he said, taking the chair she indicated.

Lauren sat on the other side of the desk and folded her hands together on the smooth surface. "And what was that?"

"I don't know. Hadn't thought much about it, but if I had . . ." He glanced around again, completing his circuit of the room where he had begun: studying her. Green eyes, as bright and true as the spring grass outside, met and held his own. Artfully applied makeup accentuated their almond shape and the delicate structure of her face. High cheekbones and a small, rounded chin made her features elfin, as though a mischievous spirit lurked behind the calm exterior.

"Something flashier," he said. "More impressive to prospective clients."

"I'm a substance person myself. And my clients come to me from referrals. If they didn't like what they'd heard, no office in the world could convince them to hire me."

"You're right."

She was good, he thought, offering her a smile. It was the megawatt one, designed to drive women to their knees. His secretary complained she only saw it when he wanted her to work late.

Lauren sat back in her chair, apparently immune to the dazzle. "Would you like some coffee?"

"Thank you, no."

Serene. That was the word he'd been looking for earlier. She was as serene and unruffled as a pond on a still summer afternoon. His gaze dipped slightly to the vee of her peach blouse. And sexy. He wasn't usually interested in women during a deal. The chase, walking the line of victory and defeat, risking everything on a single card, was more exciting than any afternoon between the sheets. Today he was distracted. The top button of her blouse exposed the hollow of her throat and a couple of inches of alabaster skin, but nothing else. Still, it was enough.

She glanced at her watch. The signal was unmistakable. He'd played cat and mouse long enough.

"I'm Jack Baldwin. I own Baldwin International. My staff recently approached you about—"

"I remember the conversation, Mr. Baldwin," she said, interrupting him. "I'm familiar with you and your company."

He leaned forward and laced his fingers together. "Then you must know that I want you."

TWO

Oh my.

Lauren stared into those blue-gray eyes and wondered what it would feel like if he really meant those words. Not that she doubted him for a minute. He *did* want her. For business. But still . . . Some tiny part of her, pushed down and ignored for perhaps too long, had quivered when he spoke.

It was chemistry, she told herself. That's all. It didn't mean anything. Besides, chemistry had been her least favorite subject in school.

"I'm not interested," she said, pleased her voice sounded calm and in control. He'd never know how close his smile had come to causing a major meltdown in the vicinity of her stomach; that if she'd been standing, her knees would have given way, causing her to land at his feet like a fallen teenage groupie.

"Why?"

"I don't have to give you a reason, Mr. Baldwin. The answer is no. Let's leave it at that."

"It's Jack." He studied her for several seconds. "I'll take that coffee now."

"Excuse me?"

He smiled again, this time a slow but cocky flash of white teeth. "You offered me coffee earlier. I'd like a cup."

"But you— I don't— Don't you have to be somewhere?"

He shook his head. "We need to talk. I think the reason you're so resistant is that you really don't know me."

"I know all about Jack Baldwin." She rose from her chair and walked over to the large, dark cabinet against the wall. Sliding back the upper doors, she exposed a narrow counter with a coffeepot and a small metal sink. "I know where you went to school and your standing in the class when you graduated. I know your father turned over the family's modestly successful company to you the day you received your M.B.A. In the last fourteen years you have parlayed that company into a multinational, multimillion-dollar giant. Your father . . ." She paused. "Oh, yes. He retired to the Bahamas, where he lives with his second wife. I know the name of your senior executives, how much your company grossed last year, before taxes, and how long you went skiing in January." She pulled open a drawer and drew out a tin of imported ground coffee. After spooning in the correct amount, she poured the water and flipped on the machine, then turned to face him. "I even know you signed a contract with the Bolasieur Company today."

His engaging smile turned into a frown. The fire in his eyes instantly iced over, and she resisted the urge to fold her arms over her chest.

"Who leaked that information?" he demanded.

"No one. The negotiations have been mentioned in the financial pages. I knew the Japanese project was next. You wouldn't be here if you hadn't finished up."

He relaxed back in his chair. "I could have lost."

"You could have, but you didn't." She raised her head and glanced out the window. "Your type never does."

"And you object to my winning?"

"No. I object to your style."

"Which is?"

Behind her the steam hissed as fresh coffee trickled into the pot. The smell filled the room and made her think of her father. The general had always demanded fresh coffee, among other things. He taught her how to find the perfect blend of beans. He'd also insisted she speak her mind. No one danced around the truth in the general's house. She had her mother's eyes and hair, but her character came from her father.

"You're a maverick."

Jack laughed and placed his hands behind his head. His right ankle rested on the opposite knee. Lauren reached for the counter pressing into the small of her back and clutched it tightly. If body language was anything to go by, he wasn't the least bit insulted by her announcement. Nor did he fear anything she had to say.

"Go on," he said. "Don't spare me."

He'd asked for it. "You're arrogant, brash, and independent. They say you're a gunslinger, but I think they're wrong. You're worse. You're a lone wolf. You do things your way or you don't do them at all. No one tells you what to do. You're a predator, Mr. Baldwin."

The limb-weakening smile was back. "I had no idea

my reputation was so . . . impressive. What exactly about all that offends you?''

"I'm not offended. I just refuse to be a part of the revolution.''

'' 'Revolution'?'' Interesting word choice. What are we—'' He chuckled. "Sorry. You're not on the team . . . yet. What am *I* revolting against?''

"I really don't see the point of discussing this further. I won't work for you.''

He rose to his feet and crossed the two feet of carpet between them in one long stride. "Wait a minute, Lauren. You can't drop all these tantalizing hints and then pull back. Wolves are dangerous animals to tease.''

"Mr. Baldwin—''

"Jack.''

He stood too close. They didn't touch, but she could feel the coiled energy of him. Heat from his body radiated out like waves of water, lapping against her resistance, soaking the edges of her resolve, until she began to forget what exactly she had objected to so strongly just a few moments before.

He *was* a wolf, all sharp instincts and predatory nature. And a loner. She had no time for a man who approached life as a game to be won.

"You want the truth?''

"Yes,'' he said, staring deeply into her eyes. It was as if he could read her thoughts and she didn't have to say a word.

His gaze flickered slightly, dropping to her mouth and she felt the energy focus and grow. Muscles in his jaw tightened. A small furrow appeared between his brows.

She parted her lips, more because she needed air than

to entice him. Instantly the heat flared hotter, brighter, as if flames licked across her cheeks, moving ever closer to her mouth. He didn't move, didn't waver in his intense attention. Her mouth trembled as though he'd brushed it with his own. But there was no physical contact. Just the sensation of being caressed, the slightly sweet taste of his breath, the damp whisper of his tongue. And still they didn't touch.

It was pheromones, she told herself. A reaction to a scent or sound. Maybe they'd known each other in a previous life. Maybe God was punishing her for cutting algebra class in high school.

"The coffee," Jack said.

"Huh?"

"I think it's ready."

"What? Oh!" She sidestepped him, then turned and reached for two mugs. "How do you like it?"

"Black."

"Of course," she murmured under her breath. "How else?" She poured the steaming liquid, then handed him a cup.

"Thanks." He moved back to his chair and sat down. "Talk to me about the revolution."

His pragmatic request, such a contrast to the intense, personal moment they had shared, destroyed the last of her lethargy. "You want to Americanize the world. It can't be done, and even if it can, it's wrong."

"Why?"

She added a teaspoon of sugar to her cup, then returned to her seat on the opposite side of the desk. "Other cultures have the right to exist and grow. To maintain their standards of life."

"What does that have to do with my contract with Tonikita Corporation?"

She shifted her weight, crossing one leg over the other. "They are a very traditional firm. The way things stand now, you won't get anywhere with them."

"That's why I want you." He placed his mug on the table and leaned forward. For the six years she'd worked at the Language Institute, she'd thought of her desk as large and sufficiently wide. But now, with Jack Baldwin stretching his long arms out towards her, the impressive width shrank to an insignificant barrier. "You're my ace in the hole."

"How flattering."

"Hey, I'm a charming kind of guy."

"So they warned me."

The problem was, they had been right. As much as he represented everything she was opposed to, and as irritating as his overdose of confidence was, she *did* find him charming in a macho kind of way. It was probably a personality flaw left over from growing up on military bases. The general would be pleased. All those manly war games had rubbed off. It didn't seem to matter that she'd spent her whole life rebelling against his way of life and everything he stood for. She and her father were too much alike for that ever to have worked. As proof, here she was being drawn in by the worst kind of maverick.

"I know what your problem is," he said.

"Oh?"

"You're tempted, and that makes you crazy."

"Mr. Baldwin—"

He raised his brows.

"Jack," she amended. "Let me assure you I'm not the least bit tempted. What you want is impossible."

"Do you know, when you lie, you get this little twitch, right here?" He touched the corner of his eye.

Instantly her hand flew up to investigate. It was only after she saw him grin that she realized she'd been had. "Okay. Maybe I was tempted. A little. But that's beside the point. We cannot work together because you don't work with anyone. I will not be a yes-man—or woman—on your staff. You don't want to be a team player, and I won't work for a dictator."

"You spend a lot of time calling me names. Have you noticed that?"

Lauren placed her elbow on the arm of the chair and rested her forehead in her hand. "How do I get rid of you?"

"Listen. That's all I ask."

"Really?"

"Yes."

"Okay. You win."

"Thanks. Number one, you may play teacher's aide all you want, Lauren Reese, but you're just hiding."

Her head snapped up. "Hiding? From what? I'll have you know that I—"

He cut her off with the shake of his head. "It's my turn. The defense gets a rebuttal at the end of the argument."

"Fine." She clenched her teeth.

"I know all about your Zen Eastern philosophy. That you only eat sacred roots or grubs or something. I don't care what you do in your free time. What I do care about is that you spent three years interning at Tonikita Corporation while you went to Tokyo University. That you belong to some *dibie* thing—"

"*Daibatsu,*" she said. "It's just a network for Tokyo University graduates. And I don't know anything about eating sacred roots."

"Whatever." He rose to his feet and began to pace

her office, stalking from window to door as though measuring out the precise number of steps would provide him with the words to convince her.

"I know about your family," he continued, holding her gaze a second before turning to pace again. "I know you spent ten years in Japan, from the time you were thirteen until you were twenty-two. I also know you've been helping some American firms negotiate contracts with Japanese companies."

"So?"

"It's all small potatoes, Lauren. You've been wanting to play the big game for a long time. This—" he motioned to include her office and the building beyond "—is just holding you back. If you weren't interested in my deal, you wouldn't have gone to so much trouble to learn everything about me."

"It's no more than you know about me."

"True." He stopped in front of her desk and placed his hands on the back of his chair. "But my staff always works up a report on a potential employee. Especially one with such an influential position." He leaned forward. "You want me, too. Face it, we could be great together. I can already feel the heat."

It was difficult to remember he was talking about a business deal. Lauren felt goose bumps puckering along her arms. Somehow, by reading a few facts and speaking with her for less than a half hour, he'd zeroed in on a problem she'd been wrestling with for more than six months. He was right; she *was* tired of teaching Japanese to college students and businessmen. Dabbling in the world of international business had been more exciting than anything in recent memory. But she'd rather have bamboo spikes driven under her nails than admit it to the arrogant man in front of her.

"What is this about my eating sacred roots?" she asked, grabbing the only safe topic from all that he'd mentioned.

"I'm not sure. It was in the staff report. Did my people take you to dinner?"

"Yes." She thought for a moment, then laughed. "I'd had a huge lunch that day. They took me to a terrific Italian restaurant on Michigan, but I only picked at a salad."

"That's how rumors get started," he said, perching on the corner of her desk. "Look at all the stories they make up about me."

"But they aren't stories."

"Lauren. You should know better than to believe everything you read."

She pushed her chair back a few inches. "You don't devour foreign companies like candy?"

"Not at all. And I never seduced the competition into signing," he said, referring to an accusation that he'd slept with a British executive's daughter just prior to a joint venture.

"I see."

"I am," he said, leaning forward, "in my own way, monogamous. The chase is my mistress."

She realized then that the rumors had all been wrong. He wasn't a cowboy or a gunslinger. He was, as she had first thought when she'd seen him in the shadows of the classroom, a warrior. If times had been different, he'd go off to war and slay the enemy. In today's modern world, that wasn't possible. Instead, business was his battlefield. He claimed contracts as booty, investments as prisoners.

"Why me?" she asked. "You said yourself that all my experiences have been with small companies. Tonikita is looking for a deal worth a hundred million. It's out of my league."

"No. It's exactly right. Baldwin International is the perfect match for them. I only need you to smooth over the edges."

"You're wrong. Mr. Yamashita has made it clear he doesn't want to deal with an American company. No one else in the States is even bothering to bid. My bet is on the Germans."

"But I have something the Germans don't have."

"What?" she asked, and then wondered how he'd found out. It explained everything.

"You. The bottom line is, you're the Japanese equivalent to a godmother for Yamashita's grandson. If you were on the team, he'd look at the deal."

The bottom line. She'd always found it such a painful expression. She still remembered the first time those words had hurt her. It had been spring in Japan, the cherry blossoms blooming with overwhelming opulence. Jiro Hattori had looked at her with his dark brown eyes. "The bottom line, kid," he'd said, "is that it won't work." She'd been so caught up in the perfect American slang coming from such classic Asian features that she'd almost missed the point of the conversation. "I'm on the executive track," he'd continued. "But I can't have an American wife. You know how those companies are."

Yeah, she knew. For three years they'd dated. She'd helped him through economics and math; he'd taught her about love. At the time, she'd tried to convince herself it had been a fair exchange. He'd married a "proper" wife within the year. She'd returned to the

States and had accepted a job with the Institute. Despite her outwardly successful life, a dark corner of her heart had never recovered from being used.

"The bottom line, Mr. Baldwin," she said, rising to her feet and walking around the desk toward the door, "is that I'm not interested. You only want me because of my connection to Yamashita."

"That's not true. You're damn good at what you do. I think you'd be successful on a larger scale. You can't deny you want the chance to try it." He moved next to her.

"That's not important. I won't work for you. Nothing has changed. You don't want a team, you want a gimmick. And I don't play that game."

He ran his hands through his thick, black hair. Confusion darkened his eyes, and she knew he was surprised by her blunt refusal.

"I don't get it," he said. "This loner stuff really bugs you."

"Absolutely."

"Would you be happier if I was some jet jocky like your dad?"

"No. That wouldn't help your cause either."

"Then what?"

"Then good-bye, Mr. Baldwin. And good luck."

He'd closed the door so quietly behind him. Lauren sighed as she remembered the soft sound. Somehow she'd thought he'd stomp out of her office, all bruised male ego and righteous anger. Instead, he'd gazed at her, the blue returning to his eyes, turning the gray into the unforgiving color of a stormy sea, then he'd nodded and left.

It was for the best, she told herself firmly as she

dropped her skirt into a pile for the dry cleaners and pulled on jeans. Good riddance and all that. But it didn't *feel* good, she thought as she slipped a sweater over her head. It didn't feel good at all.

Even as she reminded herself she had no place in her life for someone like Jack Baldwin, she acknowledged the seed of disappointment that had been growing for the last twenty-four hours. He'd disappeared without a word. Somehow she'd expected him to call or send a note, trying to win her back. There had only been silence.

After slipping her feet into leather loafers, she left her bedroom and started down the hall. The brownstone, one of hundreds in the old but pleasant neighborhood on the west side of Chicago, consisted of long, narrow rooms and thin, dark halls. The upper floors were vacant, and had been since she'd bought the place. The house had originally been built for a large family. She only needed the living area, plus one bedroom. The small den with a fireplace had been converted to an office for the evenings and weekends she brought work home.

Once in the kitchen, she started a pot of coffee, then sat down at the table in front of the window. Maybe it was time to look for a new job, she thought, gazing out toward the street. Another company, another city. With her qualifications, she could write her own ticket. She could even go back to Japan.

As quickly as that thought appeared, she pushed it away. No, she didn't want to go back to Japan. There were too many unhappy memories there. For the second time in as many days, Jiro's handsome face appeared before her. How easily she'd been taken in by his charm. His parents, both educated in the States, had encouraged him to pursue all things Western. Unfortunately for her, that had meant an American girlfriend. After seven years of struggling to fit in, Lauren had been ripe for acceptance and Jiro's practiced lines. It had never occurred to her to look past his easy smile and interest in anything or anyone American. She'd never thought that he might see her as a means to an end: a way to absorb the culture and thereby increase his value once he graduated from college.

He'd been practical; she'd been devastated. And somehow, over the last six years, she'd allowed herself to get lost inside her work, never risking her heart—never risking anything at all. So many of her choices were safe ones.

Oh, there had been men. Lauren rose from the table and poured the steaming coffee into a mug. After adding a teaspoon of sugar, she mentally recited the list of all the dates she'd had in the last several months. The number was impressive, but meaningless. She rarely accepted a second invitation. Never a third. During their weekly phone conversations, her mother inevitably brought up the fact that she wanted more grandchildren. Lauren usually reminded her that both her brothers had married and were procreating at an alarming rate. That didn't deter her mother at all. If anything, it fueled the older woman's argument about the importance of family and having people around who cared. Lauren agreed. But she'd been burned badly and wasn't ready to strike that particular match a second time. No one was going to get the chance to play her for a fool again. Which meant she should be happy that Jack Baldwin was out of her life.

The man was walking, breathing trouble. If he could

melt her bones with a single glance, imagine the devastation he could inflict with a touch. Not that they'd be anything other than business associates. He'd made it very clear he was only interested in the deal. Women came second in his life. And her only appeal was her connection to Yamashita.

A wry smile curled up the corners of her mouth. At least Jack had been brutally honest about his interest in her. There was no pretense of a relationship. Still, she couldn't help but wonder what it would be like to be the sole focus of all that energy and drive. A woman could drown in that much attention, but what a way to go.

She sipped her coffee and strolled toward the den. If she was serious about making a change, then the first order of business would be to update her resume. Then make a list of companies and start sending it out. Or maybe she should use a headhunter. There were several options to consider and—

The doorbell rang.

Lauren froze in her tracks and glanced at the clock on the wall. Seven-fifteen. On a Thursday night. Not exactly prime time for callers.

Her heart thundered loudly. She groaned as the glands throughout her body began to sway back and forth, dumping hormones into her bloodstream. Already she could feel her palms getting damp and her face flushing.

"Stop it," she said as she walked toward the door. "I don't know who it is. There's no reason to assume it's—"

But it was. Through the lace covering the center glass panel of the door, she saw the outline of a man. There was no mistaking the tall, broad silhouette. The warrior had returned for another battle. Thank God he couldn't possibly know the truth: Not only was she ready to fight the war; she was willing—no, eager—to be taken prisoner.

THREE

Jack rang the bell again, then glanced at the trio of children staring at him. They sat on their bikes, feet braced on the sidewalk. Ever since he'd parked his car in front of the brownstone, they'd watched him like silent sentinels. He knew his low-slung black sports car was out of place in this family neighborhood, but that was no reason for them to treat him like a two-headed monster.

"Evening," he said, nodding in their direction.

The oldest, a boy of about ten, grinned. "Hi. Lauren's home. I saw her drive in about an hour ago. Sometimes she takes a while to answer the door, though. If the stereo's on, she can't hear nothin'."

"Thanks."

How did this munchkin know so much about Lauren's personal habits? he wondered. He was about to press the bell again when a shadow flashed across the glass panel from the inside. There was the click of a lock being released, then the door swung open.

"Mr. Baldwin," she said, her voice raised slightly with surprise.

He grinned. "I thought we'd solved that particular problem."

"You're right. Jack. I wasn't expecting you. I thought we'd said everything at my office yesterday."

He leaned against the doorframe and studied the soft mahogany hair tumbling over her shoulders. "That just goes to show, you think too much. May I come in?"

"Sure." She stepped back.

"Hey, Lauren," that same boy called.

"Hi, Billy," she said, waving.

"Should I tell my mom you said hello?"

She glanced quickly at Jack, then back out the door, and sighed. "Damn," she said softly, then louder, "Yes, Billy. Tell her hello and that I'll call her this weekend."

"Okay. 'Bye." He and his friends turned and pedaled away.

"Should I have shown them my driver's license?" he asked.

"Who?"

"The three bodyguards out front. They glared at me like I was an escapee from the local prison."

"Oh, Terry, Billy's mom, and I are friends. She worries about my being on my own. Billy knows that and sometimes takes it upon himself to watch out for me. The kids were probably just curious about a strange man, ah . . ." She looked up at him, her green eyes flashing with irritation and something that might have been embarrassment. "Not to imply I never have strange men here. Well, not strange, but I do go out and . . ." She paused.

"Yes?" he offered helpfully.

"That is to say . . . Could we change the subject?"

"Sure. No problem." He started to slip off his leather jacket, then remembered the package. "Here," he said, thrusting it at her. "They're for you."

She opened the brown bag and pulled out a carton of Chinese food. "What on earth did you bring me?"

"Egg rolls." He tossed his jacket on the wing chair standing at a right angle to the sofa. "Vegetarian, just in case you do have some secret need to eat sacred roots."

"Egg rolls?"

"Yeah. Haven't you had them before?" He took the box from her hands and opened it. "There's a place down by the office. A little hole in the wall. I wanted to bring something as a peace offering, but couldn't decide what. As I was driving home, I passed the restaurant and realized they made the perfect gift."

"Egg rolls?" she repeated.

"You keep saying that. Here." He picked up one of the golden brown treats and held it to her lips. "Try it."

Their eyes met. There it was again. He'd felt it in her office. That arc of awareness, like an electric shock, jolted through his body. They weren't even touching and already he could sense the change in her breathing. And in his own. Lauren Reese might be all Zen calm and one hundred percent business on the surface, but there was a fire smoldering underneath—he had the burns to prove it.

"Just a taste," he murmured, lowering his gaze to her mouth.

She parted her lips slightly as small white teeth bit down on the egg roll. She chewed slowly, as though savoring the blended flavors and mixed textures. A tiny crumb of flaky crust clung to the corner of her mouth. Before he could say anything, or brush it off himself, her tongue moved across her lower lip and swept it away. Heat raced through him.

"How was it?" he asked.

"Delicious. No one's brought egg rolls as a gift before."

"Then I'm your first?"

"I . . ." Her gaze skittered away, then back. "Yes. Thank you."

"I wanted to apologize for walking out of your office yesterday. It was very unprofessional of me."

"No," she said, never taking her eyes from his. "It's my fault. I should have been more willing to listen. Sometimes I get stuck in one place and it's hard to move forward."

"Does that mean you'll talk to me now?"

"Yes."

She'd washed away her makeup, leaving her skin pale and clear. Freckles marched across her nose and cheeks, making her look young and vulnerable. Tiny lines fanned out from the corners of her eyes. He'd seen them deepen when she smiled. They marked the passage of time and reminded him she was very much a woman. He could smell the lingering scent of her perfume blending with the unique fragrance of her body. The two combined with the smell of the food to create an irresistible combination.

Jack moved a half step closer, until he could feel her heat. Her earlier reluctant confession told him that while she might date, there wasn't anyone serious in her life. He forced the thought—and the pleasure it gave him—from his mind. This attraction wasn't part of his plan at all. He never got involved when he was into a deal. It wasn't a rule; it didn't have to be. Once the work began, he wasn't interested in women. His mistress, as he had told Lauren yesterday, was the chase.

"There's more," he said, offering the egg roll again.

"What about you?"

"What do you mean?"

"Don't you want something?" She flushed, the color climbing across her cheeks until it blended with the freckles. "I can't finish them all by myself."

"That's very generous." He bit down exactly where she had, savoring the crisp shell, then the soft but crunchy center. He imagined he could taste her flavor, the touch of unexpected sweetness that lingered on his lips.

"I have coffee," she said, then turned and fled the room.

Jack grinned and finished the egg roll, then wiped his fingers and glanced around the room. It was much as he'd expected, all soft colors with elegant, but comfortable, furniture. Peach and cream blended together in the print on the chairs and matched the muted wallpaper.

In the far corner stood a tall metal sculpture. He moved closer. The black metal lines rose toward the heavens in a representation of a bird breaking free of the earth. One wing stretched out, taut, powerful; the other folded into the base of the piece, mired in the cold reality of steel. The passion and depth of the artwork caused him to frown and look away. He felt like a voyeur. Intellectually he knew Lauren displayed the sculpture because she liked it and wanted others to enjoy it; emotionally he wondered if she knew it exposed her soul.

"Here," she said, walking back into the room carrying a tray. "I'd made a fresh pot before you arrived." She followed the line of his vision. "I see you've noticed my bird." She smiled and set the tray on the coffee table in front of the sofa. "I bought it in Japan, about two months before I left. I'd seen it in a gallery. The artist is French." She moved next to him and gently touched the bird's outstretched wing.

He wanted to ask if she'd broken free of whatever had held her down. If she'd recovered from the tragedy that shadowed her eyes and caused her mouth to tremble. He wanted to pull her close, surround her with his strength, and promise to keep her safe always.

The rush of needs, all foreign, all unwelcome, caused him to step back and take the seat farthest from her. What the hell was wrong with him? He was here to convince her to join his company and help him negotiate a hundred-million-dollar contract. Nothing more. He wasn't interested in a woman like Lauren Reese. She was the kind looking for home and hearth, a baseball team worth of kids and a few dozen pets. And a husband. He was looking for the next deal. He'd learned early on, business was all he could count on. People came and went, but the deal would never leave him. His part-time lovers accommodated their schedules to his, and right now he was too busy to play bed-buddies with anyone.

Lauren sat in the center of the couch and handed him a cup of coffee. "Black, I believe you said yesterday."

"Thanks." He took the mug, careful to avoid touching her, then leaned back in the wing chair. "What changed your mind?"

"About talking to you?"

He nodded.

"It's time for me to move on. And you're right."
She smiled. "I am tempted by the challenge. But don't
think I'm going to be a pushover, Jack Baldwin. If we
can work out a mutually agreeable arrangement, I'll
help you with the Tonikita contract, but only as an
employee. I will not use my relationship with Kiyoshi
Yamashita to any advantage. And if you don't like
those terms—"

"Fine," he said, interrupting her.

"That's it?" She flipped her hair away from her
face and over her shoulders, then leaned back on the
sofa. "Golly, I thought you'd put up at least token
resistance."

"I need you," he said, setting the cup on the table.
"We both know that."

Lauren looked at him. Her green eyes darkened, and
he saw her swallow. His hands closed into fists as his
fingers itched to stroke the smooth skin of her throat.
Get a grip, he told himself angrily. This was business,
dammit. He was a man, not some randy preteen in the
backseat of his father's car.

He shifted in the chair, then forced himself to relax.
"I might be a . . . What was it you called me?"

"Lone wolf?"

"Yeah. I might be a lone wolf, but I'm not a fool.
I know enough about the Japanese market to realize I
need an expert, and I think you're that person."

He was willing to accept her rule of not using her
family connection with Yamashita. After all, the old
man would see her name on the correspondence. That
would be enough to get Baldwin International in the
door. After that, he'd be fine on his own. He always
had been.

"I'll need to get a leave of absence from the Institute," she said.

"Is that a problem?"

"No. It's in my employment agreement. They like us to do outside contracting. It means more business for them."

"How?"

She smiled. "If you get the deal with Tonikita, a large portion of your staff will need to become fluent in Japanese. Where else would you send them?"

"Maybe I'll hire you permanently and you can tutor them."

She looked quickly away. "Let's take one arrangement at a time."

He'd upset her. That much was clear. But why? The rapid rise and fall of her chest indicated the increase in her rate of breathing. Her sweater, loosely knit and the color of morning fog, slipped off one shoulder, exposing creamy skin, a few darker dots that could only be freckles, and a lacy peach strap that made him think about tracing the frilly edge down to the hidden, soft, feminine curves.

Reluctantly drawing his attention away from the alluring sight and vowing to ignore the reaction making itself known against the button fly of his jeans, he reached for his mug.

"How long until you can start with Baldwin International? The bids are only being accepted for a few weeks."

"I can be there Monday."

"Are you sure?"

She nodded. "I can work over the weekend to clear up anything at the Institute. You can have your financial people get going on the proposal."

"They already are."

"You were *that* sure?"

"Yes." He chuckled and took a sip of coffee. "I knew that once you got to know me, you wouldn't turn down the opportunity."

"Uh-huh. Speaking of which, there are a few parameters we need to cover."

"Such as?"

"We play by my rules or we don't play."

"Isn't that a little presumptuous?" he asked. "What makes you think your rules are better?"

"I know Yamashita. If you go in there with both barrels blazing, you'll end up blowing yourself right out of the water."

Jack rested one ankle on the opposite knee and grinned. "That's quite an assumption."

"It is your usual style. You tend to overwhelm your competition and potential partners with information, unwavering determination, and a very aggressive stance." She leaned forward as she spoke, absently pulling up the dropping neckline of her sweater. "You can't do this alone, Jack. You're right. You *do* need me. And if you don't listen, you'll fail."

Conviction burned in her eyes with all the intensity of a martyr facing the devil. He knew the feeling. "I won't believe the negotiators can't listen to a few facts without getting their panties in a bunch."

"It's not what you say, it's how you say it. More than that, it's how you walk and the words you choose. Even the way you speak tells everybody who and what you are." Her hands danced in time with her speech, flashing her sincerity, reaching out to beseech him.

"And who am I?"

He'd meant to ask the question lightly, to tease her into laughter, to force the rising tension from the room. Instead, the low, husky question hung between them like a pulsing beacon illuminating their—he realized now—mutual attraction.

Her hands grew still. The sweater slipped again. In the soft lamplight, her skin glowed as though lit from within. He longed to touch the creamy flesh, to taste and savor it.

"A wolf," she murmured, as though the words had become difficult to speak.

"Who should I be?"

Her eyes dilated, darkening the green until the colors blended into twin bottomless pools. She moistened her lips. "I'm not sure."

"You know. Tell me."

"A . . . a warrior."

"A samurai?"

"Yes."

"Why?"

"You must learn to use their energy against them."

He shook his head and leaned forward. "I don't understand."

"Your way, the Western way, is for one man to stand alone. That's not bad, but the one man is taught to meet his enemies head-on." She scooted down the couch, toward him. "You push. If it doesn't work the first time, you push harder." She made a fist with her right hand and hit it against the palm of her left.

"What should I do?"

"Use their energy against them. Steal the motion and make it your own." She reached out and took his hand. The current crackled between them as though two live wires had become entangled. Holding his hand out, she pressed her fist against the palm. "See, there is no success, for either of us. We could push against each other all night. And nothing would be gained."

He wasn't sure he agreed with her assessment of the situation. Something was being gained. For him, at least. He could inhale the scent of her body, feel the heat of her hand wrapped so firmly around his wrist. And her mouth . . .

The soft cupid's-bow curve of her lips was only inches from his own. Treacherous thoughts invaded. Reminding himself it was a business meeting didn't seem to help.

"I should use your energy against you?" he asked. "So this is like karate?"

"Yes. Are you familiar with the sport?"

"No." He forced himself to smile as if her closeness were merely interesting. "I jog, play racquetball, work out at the gym."

She frowned. "Either solitary or aggressive activities. We have a lot to work on."

"But see how well I've learned the first lesson."

"What do you—"

He tugged on the fist pressed against his. Before Lauren could brace herself, she was already moving off the sofa and into his lap. Strong hands turned her so she landed on her fanny. Her first thought was that his thighs were as firm and strong as molded steel. Her second was that she had to get away as fast as she could. She pushed against his chest, but he held her still.

Their eyes met. As quickly as a rising summer storm,

the blue fled his irises, leaving behind flickering gray flame. Long, dark lashes cast half-moon shadows on his cheekbones.

"Jack?"

"Aren't you going to reward me for learning my lesson?"

"This isn't a good idea. I work for you. Neither of us mixes business with pleasure."

"Agreed."

"Then let me go."

"So you admit it's pleasurable?"

His arms surrounded her, drawing her ever closer to his body. She could see the individual whiskers shadowing his cheeks and jaw. The line of his mouth, normally firm and businesslike, softened slightly as if he were already anticipating some forbidden fruit.

"Yes," she whispered, glancing at the long fingers slipping under the cuff of her sweater and rubbing against her bare skin. Her hands, only seconds ago so intent on pushing away, surrendered to the moment. They crept up and clung to his powerful shoulders. She could feel his strength—and his gentleness.

"You don't start work until Monday," he said. "Right now we are simply a man and a woman fighting a powerful attraction."

"That's just semantics. It doesn't change the fact that we *will* work together."

"Don't you know some of the finest lawyers in this country make a terrific living based on semantics? As for the rest of it . . . Ah hell, Lauren, your red hair and stubborn streak would tempt a saint. And we've already established what I am."

"I thought—"

"Don't." His hand cupped her head and urged her closer. "Don't think. Just feel."

Of its own accord, her chin tilted and she met him more than halfway. Those brief miniseconds when she'd allowed herself to imagine kissing Jack Baldwin, she'd assumed his seduction would be all assault and plunder. A fast and hazardous ride toward the heavens.

Instead he attacked with stealth and subtlety. Soft pressure covered her mouth, followed by a gentle back-and-forth motion. He threaded his fingers through her hair, caressing the back of her neck. The other hand rested on her hip. The slight weight, a searing heat that burned through her jeans and could have easily been pushed away, anchored her in place as though metal shackles bound her legs.

She responded in kind, moving her lips slightly against his, tasting the coffee and something else. It was Jack, his own flavor, almost familiar, as though they'd kissed before, or as if her body had known and prepared for this moment. There had been others, she told herself. Other kisses, other men. He wasn't any different. Even as she thought the lie, she dismissed it. This felt different. It felt right.

He whispered her name softly, then nibbled along her jaw. He found the sensitive spot under her ear and pressed the tip of his tongue to the pulse beating there. She arched toward him, thrusting her breasts against his chest.

He was, in his own fashion, a gentleman, she thought hazily, as the hand remained on her hip. The invitation, offered instinctively, had been ignored. He returned to her mouth, his tongue tracing back and forth along her lower lip. She parted to admit him.

At the first touch of his tongue, she felt the shivers

slip down her spine. He withdrew, then returned. At the second touch, the electricity raced through her body, causing her muscles to clench and release in rapid-fire sequence. Her fingers reached for the soft silk of his black hair; her hips shifted, looking for proof that his need matched her own. And still his tongue teased in guerrilla warfare, never entering for more than a second, touching and retreating, making her long for them to mate, lips sealed as they explored and tasted, taught and excited. Their breathing grew rapid.

But he knew, as she did, that if they dared pass the invisible line, all control would be lost.

At last, when she knew she couldn't stand another second of his game, he straightened and leaned his head back against the chair. Gray eyes studied her. He reached for her hand, still caught in his hair, and tugged it until he captured her fingers in his own. Then he kissed her palm.

"I didn't mean for that to happen," he said softly. "But I'm glad it did. We both wondered."

"I—" Lauren started to deny his statement, then realized her reaction to his touch told its own truth. "It can't happen again."

"I know." He smiled. "The chase is a very jealous mistress. If I'm unfaithful, she has a way of messing up the deal."

The deal. She fought back a sigh. How could she have allowed herself to forget what was really important to Jack Baldwin? She was simply a means to an end. He was using her, as Jiro had. This time the tactic had been exposed up front, so if her heart got bruised, she only had herself to blame. Jack had made it very clear what he wanted from her. The fact that she found him intriguing was her own problem. So what if their kiss had felt so right? When the contract with Tonikita was signed, he would move on to the next project. She would be as memorable as the fax machine.

She felt the brush of his thumb on her palm. Okay, maybe slightly more memorable than office equipment, but she was a fool if she expected anything lasting from him.

She pulled her hand free and slid off his lap to her feet. Moving to the far side of the room, she crossed her arms over her chest. "Then I have your word?"

The muscles in his jaw tightened slightly, and she wondered if the cause was irritation or regret.

"Yes, Lauren. From now on, business only. And by your rules. Tell me what to do and I'll do it."

He sounded sincere; she knew better. "How do you do that?"

"What?"

"Lie so easily. Rules, my ass. You're going to fight me every step of the way. You're going to challenge me and make fun of the changes and generally make my life hell."

He rose to his feet and grinned. "Maybe. But I want this contract more than I've ever wanted anything. So you might be surprised at my willingness to compromise."

"I'll believe it when I see it."

She studied his tall, broad body. If only . . . Yeah, right. In the last six years, she'd spent too much time fighting the "if onlys." It was time to get on with her life. Jack Baldwin was using her to get a contract. She could use him as well. The experience with his firm would give her an in to the power players. She'd been wrestling with the idea of a change. Here it was, staring her in the face. The fact that it came packaged in a gorgeous six-foot-three-inch frame was a detail that she'd deal with another time. So what if she found him attractive? And charming. Nothing was going to happen between them. He was more interested in the contract than her.

But the pragmatic realization didn't make her feel any better.

"This won't work," she said, voicing her doubts out loud.

"Of course it will." He shrugged on his black leather jacket. "I've never failed before. Don't even know the meaning of the word."

"So you always get what you want?"

His gaze held hers, then dropped to her mouth. For a heartbeat, she felt the tangible caress against her lips. "Always."

"That's pretty arrogant, even for you."

He walked to the door. "Not really. I got you, didn't I?" He winked. "Monday, Lauren. Prepare to meet the wolf in his lair."

FOUR

Lauren had never actually seen a wolf's lair before, but she doubted that predators usually lived in a downtown Chicago high-rise. She stood across the street from the steel and glass structure and tilted her head back to try and see to the top. The crowd of morning commuters surged around her. Somewhere in that maze of offices was Baldwin International. If she knew Jack, the company would be located on the upper floors, more for the prestige than because he cared about the view.

Her work at the Language Institute had wrapped up quickly—too quickly. She'd had ample time to regret her hasty decision. The fact that this was a terrific opportunity, and that she'd be well on her way if she pulled it off, didn't keep her stomach from knotting up or her knees from trembling. She could fall on her butt. It would be a very public failure. If Baldwin International was turned down during preliminary negotiations—and with Jack's reputation, that was more than likely—people would say she couldn't cut it with the high rollers.

So why was she putting herself through this? He'd hired her to get an in with Yamashita. She'd be crazy to think he'd actually listen to anything she was going to say. Despite his promise to go by her rules, it was going to be a disaster. If she was smart, she'd walk right back to the Language Institute, call Jack, and say she'd changed her mind. Another chance would come along, a safer one.

Even as she rehearsed the words she'd use to explain her change of heart, she could hear her father lecturing her on the fine points of not giving up. *Don't start what you don't intend to finish.*

It's not me, Daddy, she thought. *It's Jack. He'll never follow my suggestions.*

It's fear, came the answering echo.

All right, so she was scared. No big deal. That didn't mean a timely retreat wouldn't— No! She was committed to this new road. She'd survive it and make the situation work for her. Or *she'd* end up committed.

She groaned softly at the bad pun, then took a deep breath. On the sidewalk, someone jostled her. She clutched her briefcase more tightly, stepped out into the street and toward the building.

Forty floors above ground level, the elevator door swished open. Lauren stepped into the foyer of Baldwin International and approached the receptionist. The first day on a new job always reminded her of the first day of school. She'd worn her favorite suit for luck, but that didn't stop her from remembering those terrifying moments when she'd walked into her first classroom in Japan. At thirteen she'd been all long legs and arms.

A gangly colt in a room full of graceful Oriental flowers. Her bright red hair had shone like a beacon, her freckles seemed to glow in the morning sun. She'd been different, and barely able to speak the language.

She shook off the memory. This wasn't Japan, and she was all grown-up. She smiled at the young woman sitting at the console of phones.

"Good morning. I'm Lauren Reese. I believe—"

"Welcome to Baldwin International," the blonde interrupted. "Mr. Baldwin has been expecting you." She glanced over her shoulder, as if checking to see if the coast was clear. Her large gold earrings jingled with the movement. "He's been pacing back and forth, calling me every three minutes to see if you're here, but I'm not supposed to tell you that."

"Really?"

"Oh, sure." Red lips smiled again. "So you're somebody important, aren't you?"

"Well, I—"

"I know, be modest. It suits you. Have a seat." With that, she pressed a button using one long, manicured finger and spoke into her headset. "Ms. Reese is here, Mr. Baldwin." She looked up. "He'll be right out."

Lauren nodded her thanks. She slowly scanned the room, taking in the Hockney prints and long, leather couches. The waiting area was what she expected; the receptionist was not. Somehow she'd thought Jack would employ a conservative-looking person to man the front desk. The flashy blonde with her low-cut blouse and sultry voice didn't fit with what she knew about his operation.

Before she could decide which of the overstuffed

sofas to perch on, a door swung open and Jack strode toward her.

She'd spent the entire weekend telling herself that the sparks between them had been the result of her overactive imagination and nothing more.

She'd been wrong—her stomach dove for her toes—very wrong.

Every tall, broad, masculine inch of him exuded power and confidence. The office was his home turf, and he moved with the grace and style of someone to the manor born. He had been, she reminded herself. He'd inherited Baldwin International at the tender age of twenty-four. He'd probably learned to read with the *Wall Street Journal* as his primer.

He'd removed his suit jacket and, despite the fact that it wasn't quite nine in the morning, already rolled up his shirt sleeves to the elbow. The finely woven white cotton contrasted with the tan on his arms and the sprinkling of dark hairs. Wool trousers emphasized long legs and narrow hips. His megawatt grin threatened her balance. When he reached her and held out his hand to shake, she prepared herself for the impact.

Palm touched palm. Fingers brushed. Hard on soft, smooth on rough. His clean and virile scent surrounded her like a warm cloak, sensitizing her body until her skin whimpered for more.

Their eyes met. It wasn't the car crash she'd been expecting. No, seeing Jack again was more like a quiet explosion, scattering her senses and leaving her worried about the effort required to string sentences together.

"Good morning." His low words, simple and correct under the circumstances, broke through her momentary stupor.

"Hello." One word. Good start. Next time she'd

add another, then another, until she formed an entire sentence. She could do this.

She tried to retrieve her hand. He held it fast. The blue faded from his irises, leaving behind smoky gray. Long fingers squeezed slightly, then he released her.

From start to finish, the encounter had lasted less than thirty seconds. Lauren swallowed and shifted her briefcase from one side to the other. She was expected to work with this man? So much for wishing the attraction had all been the workings of an overtired brain.

"I'm glad you're here," he said.

After the handshake, his unexpected admission landed like the second blow of a one-two punch and forced her to respond in kind. "Thanks." She spoke softly, then cleared her throat and tried again. "Trying to find common ground between Baldwin International and Tonikita Corporation should be a challenge." That was better. She sounded more like a professional and less like a woman on the verge of surrender.

The blue returned to his eyes, toning down the flames. "And you never walk away from a challenge?"

"I try not to."

"That's my philosophy, too. So we have something in common?"

"Yes," she said firmly. "Business."

The right side of his mouth curved up, exposing his dimple and her lie. He glanced over her shoulder at the woman sitting behind the reception desk, then back at her. "Why don't we start with the nickel tour?"

"Great."

"This is Annie."

Lauren turned and smiled. "We've met, in a manner of speaking, but good morning."

Annie waggled her red-tipped fingers. "Greetings."

"This way." Jack placed his hand on the small of Lauren's back and guided her out the door he'd entered. As they walked down the hallway, she gritted her teeth and tried to ignore the subtle pressure urging her forward. Little bullets of heat shot into her bloodstream.

"Annie's not our regular receptionist. Cathy's on vacation, and Annie's filling in."

Lauren nodded. That made sense. "Is Annie a temp?"

"No. She handles entertainment for our European clients. She's fun and outgoing, and they enjoy that. She arranges dinners and whatever else they'd like."

Lauren stopped and stared. "You're kidding."

One long finger touched the bottom of her chin and forced her mouth closed. "You have a dirty mind," he said. "No, not sex. Tickets to the theater, walking tours of the museums, box seats at the Cubs games."

"I knew that." Heat climbed her cheeks.

"Sure."

The long, carpeted hallway ended in a large, open work area. Half a dozen secretaries looked up and smiled as they walked through. Jack introduced her.

"I'd tell you their names, but I know it's tough to keep everyone straight," he said, perching on the corner of a desk. "Better for you to learn as you go. The general secretarial work is handled here, but you'll have your own staff."

"That will be helpful."

Her calm words belied her shock. Based on everything she'd seen and heard about him, she'd assumed he'd shove her in a back room somewhere. One of the women asked him a question. He looked at the papers she offered and studied them.

While they discussed the problem, Lauren watched

the other secretaries. One or two looked at Jack with unconcealed lust, but the rest were busy with their work. The slight charge in the atmosphere seemed to come from interest and excitement rather than fear. She'd thought Jack would make a tyrannical boss, but maybe her second assumption was as wrong as the first.

He gave a last couple of instructions, then rose. "Your office is through here." He motioned for her to circle around the desks. "I gave you a window."

"I'm flattered."

"You earned it."

"I haven't started working yet. How could I have earned it?"

"You got me in with Tonikita Corporation."

"You've already heard back from them?"

"No." He grinned. "But we both know they're going to say yes."

Because of her. Lauren tried to quell the wave of disappointment. For a few minutes she'd allowed herself to forget why she was here. Oh sure, some of it was that she was damn good at her job. But mostly it was because she was godmother to Yamashita's first and only grandchild. Family ties were all-important to the Japanese patriarch. Jack was right; as soon as word got out she was part of the package, Baldwin International would be invited to bid. Best for her and her employer to remember exactly where they both stood. If only he hadn't kissed her.

"This way." Jack stepped into yet another corridor. He walked in front, pointing out different departments, the library, copy and fax rooms. She kept up easily, telling herself she could think better without his hand burning a hole through her back. That she didn't miss his casual touch. That she was insane to hope the attraction was mutual.

"How much space does your company have in this building?" she asked.

"Three floors. The other two are directly below." He glanced over his shoulder. "Why are you smiling like that?"

"Somehow I guessed you'd be on the top floor."

He paused, then turned until he was standing directly in front of her. The hallway narrowed slightly. As an employee passed them, they were forced to crowd together. The heat flared instantly.

"Have I been insulted?" he asked.

He didn't touch her. He didn't have to. His voice seduced her for him, whispering along her hands and face, slipping under her suit jacket to caress her bare arms.

"I just meant—"

"I know."

They stared at each other for several more heartbeats. Lauren reminded herself about why she was here, repeated to herself that he was only using her, and that she was going to try using him back. She told herself this temporary job was simply a stepping-stone to new heights in her career.

It didn't help. She was being drawn in by a force she'd never encountered before; something strong and powerful, beyond her capability to resist. She *should* have turned back when she had the chance; now it was too late. She was caught in a trap of her own making.

As quickly as it had flared, the heat subsided to a manageable level. Jack frowned slightly, then resumed leading the way toward her office.

"Beth is your secretary; Sally, your assistant," he

said. "There's a list of all the phone numbers you should need, an organizational chart to tell you the players. I've set up a couple of introductory meetings for later this afternoon. You can get to know the members of the team."

Surprise, surprise. So he did plan on making her work. Perhaps he wanted her for more than her relationship with Yamashita. She hoped so. She wanted this job to be successful. Not only because Jack could tickle her toes with just a look, but because she needed the win in her life. She'd been coasting too long.

They passed through a set of open double doors. There wasn't any sign hanging on the wall, but she knew they'd entered the executive sanctum.

"Over here," Jack said, pointing to an alcove on the left. He stepped aside and allowed her to precede him.

What she had thought was a small corner actually opened up into a good-sized waiting area. A desk and a leather couch dominated the room. Three plants were grouped together in one corner. A steaming cup of coffee and a pushed-back chair indicated that her secretary would be returning soon.

"Beth is probably collecting files," he said. "Come meet Sally."

Past the first room was a slightly larger office. A petite, dark-haired woman rose from behind her desk and smiled. There was a look of intelligence and welcome in her brown eyes. "Hi. I'm Sally Fischer." She held out her hand. "I'm pleased to be working for you. I've been part of the research team on the Tonikita Corporation project, so let me know what information you'll need."

Lauren shook her hand. "Thank you. I will."

"Sally speaks Japanese," Jack said, moving closer to the two women.

Sally laughed. "Hardly. I'm taking a class. I can say hello and good-bye, plus the weird things they teach you. My pencil is under the desk, that sort of thing."

"It's useful if you actually *drop* your pencil."

Sally grimaced. "What I'd need is more along the lines of 'I'm sorry I spilled my coffee in your lap.' Jack says you're fluent."

"I went to high school and college in Tokyo. I learned to speak the language as a way to survive. I never quite fit in physically, though." She pointed to her red hair.

"At least it made you easy to spot in a crowd."

"That's true. My family could always keep track of me when we went out. But I used to wish for black hair and brown eyes. The kids teased me that I had Godzilla eyes."

A low male chuckle reminded her that Jack was still in the room. For a few seconds she'd managed to forget about him. She groaned silently. Childhood reminiscences were not the most professional thing to share on the first day of work.

"Come here." He motioned for her to enter the next door. "As promised, a window."

She walked into her office. The pale walls and carpet made the large space seem even bigger. Open vertical blinds allowed the morning sunlight to filter onto the large oak desk. A computer monitor sat on the right, bookshelves on the left. But it was the small green plant on the corner of her desk that caught her attention.

"A bonsai tree?" she asked.

He shrugged and walked over to the desk. "I just wanted to welcome you aboard."

She approached the trimmed plant. Dark shavings covered the soil. A tiny ceramic wise man leaned on a spindly cane next to a miniature white bridge.

She'd expected the charm, had half hoped for the attraction. She'd even been looking forward to locking horns with his aggressive Western style of business. But she'd never expected him to be . . . nice. Most bosses wouldn't have bothered with anything. A small percentage would have ordered a generic floral arrangement. This perfect miniature showed Jack had thought the gift through, maybe even bought it himself. If he'd meant to disarm her, he couldn't have found a better way.

"Thank you, Jack." She reached out impulsively, then pulled her hand back. Better for them not to touch. "It's lovely. The office, the staff, the plant. I couldn't be happier."

He folded his arms over his chest. "Hang on to that feeling, Godzilla-eyes. We have our first meeting on Wednesday. And you know what that means."

"Trouble?"

"Absolutely. Because I *will* have my way."

She dropped her briefcase onto her chair and placed her hands on her hips. "Have you forgotten already? We agreed. My rules. I tell you what to do and you do it."

Blue-gray eyes gleamed with amusement, but his face held on to a straight expression. "That never happened."

"I knew it! You were lying!"

"A man's gotta do what a man's gotta do."

"Not on my time, mister!"

Jack leaned one hip against her desk. "What are you going to do about it?"

"Fight you on your own terms. Aggressively prove that I'm right." She moved closer. They were almost at eye level. "If you want this deal, it will have to happen my way."

"I'm the boss." His voice lowered slightly.

"I'm the expert."

"Maybe."

"Maybe?" She glared at him. "I'll have you know that I'm worth every penny you're paying me."

"How much is that, by the way?"

She named an outrageous sum.

"I'll notify personnel." He straightened and walked to the door, then turned to face her. "But be warned. I'll make you earn it."

"That's what I'm here to do. Close the deal and walk away."

His gaze moved quickly from the top of her head down to her toes, then back. She shivered; the predator had returned.

"I agree with the first," he said. "As to the second, let's talk about that when the contracts are signed."

Jack stood and stretched. After rubbing his eyes, he glanced at the clock on his computer screen and groaned. Past eight already. He'd been at the office over twelve hours today. It felt like twenty, and he hadn't made a dent in the pile of work on his desk. The time in New York had put him behind. But it had been worth it. He allowed himself a smile of satisfaction. News of his deal with the French company had spread quickly. Three headhunters had called offering prime executive talent for sale, and some investment bankers were making noises about taking Baldwin International public. They'd make him rich, they promised.

He loosened his tie and pulled it free. He was already rich—and in control. It didn't get much better than that.

After turning off the computer, he picked up his suit jacket and slung it over one shoulder. He stuffed the tie into his pants pocket and left the room.

The unseasonably warm Chicago spring day had darkened into evening. There would be a cold spell or two before summer officially arrived, but for this week, temperatures had climbed into the high seventies. It was the perfect night for a jog along the lakefront. Or dinner with a beautiful woman.

As he walked into the hall, his gaze automatically went to the last door on the left. In two days he'd already picked up the habit of watching for Lauren. Since he'd gotten her settled in her office, he hadn't seen her. Not for want of trying. He'd walked past her end of the corridor about five times a day, hoping for a glimpse. He felt like a teenager cruising the halls for his girl. He hadn't acted that way since . . . He shook his head. He couldn't remember when. He'd been packed off to boarding school after his mother had died when he was twelve. No girls there. College? Maybe. But he'd been so busy keeping his grades up and playing sports, there hadn't been a lot of extra time. He'd dated enough to learn about the unique differences between a man and a woman, but not enough to get rid of the feeling he was the only person in his life whom he could depend on to be there for the short and the long haul.

All that didn't explain his hormone problem where Lauren was concerned. She was just a woman, he told himself. Nothing special at all. Beautiful, intelligent females were his normal style. He didn't need to see her. In fact, he was done thinking about her. He would go home and relax, maybe invite a friend over for dinner.

He was about to turn toward the elevator when he spotted a sliver of light shining out from under Lauren's closed door. She must have left it on. She couldn't still be working.

He walked past her assistant's desk. Knocking and pushing the door open at the same time, he moved into her office.

"Lauren?"

She looked up and smiled. "Hi. You're working late." Large-framed glasses perched on her nose.

"I could say the same about you."

"I'm trying to impress the boss," she said. "What's your excuse?"

"I *am* the boss. The buck stops with me." He sat in the leather chair in front of her desk. "I was only joking about having to earn your keep here. I'm not a slave driver."

"I know. But I'm enjoying myself. I didn't want to stop." She pushed her glasses up on top of her head.

"I didn't know you wore glasses."

"Just for reading."

"Aren't you a little young?"

"I'm farsighted. Have been since I was a kid." She grimaced and leaned back in her chair. "What a sight. Red hair, freckles, and glasses. You can imagine how the boys swarmed over me."

"You forgot the Godzilla eyes."

His gaze drifted to her hair. She'd pulled the long, mahogany tresses into a neat bun. A few wisps escaped to tease her cheeks and neck. Green eyes, framed by dark lashes, watched him watch her. The lipstick had long faded from her mouth, but that didn't keep him from remembering the kiss they'd shared at her house. He licked his lower lip as if he could still taste her.

Trying to change the direction of his thoughts, he moved his eyes lower. A conservative blouse, the color of a sunrise, draped over her delicate shoulders and hid her breasts from view. Yesterday her suit had been a deep green; today it was chestnut. He liked her in a suit. He smiled. He'd liked her in that sweater better. There was something to be said for an unexpected view of lingerie. Even if it was just a bra strap. He'd been wrong. There was something special about Lauren. It wasn't her clothes or her looks or even her perfume. It was her.

He tossed his jacket on the desk. "I don't think the boys ignored you for that long. If they did, they were foolish."

A shadow passed over her face. "You forget I went to high school in Japan. Their beauty ideal doesn't lend itself to carrot tops." Traces of the past tightened her mouth.

He wanted to ask who had hurt her, but that was too personal a question. God knew he hated to talk about *his* past. Besides, they were to be strictly business. "I can't believe there wasn't at least one who saw the potential," he said softly.

She shrugged. "Ancient history. Are you sitting in on the seminar tomorrow?"

The change of subject was anything but subtle. He let her slide. "Of course."

"I saw the memo you sent out. Talk about a command performance." She laughed, relaxing in her seat. "I was going to say you *practically* ordered everyone to attend, but there is no practically about it. It was a direct order."

"It's important for my people to hear you out."

"I know, but you could have told them a little more gently."

He rested one ankle on his opposite knee. "Complaining about my management style after just two days?"

She moved her pens and pencils until they lined up neatly. "Of course not."

"You've got that twitch back."

"What twitch?"

"The one right here." He pointed to the corner of his eye. "You get it when you lie."

She reached up to touch her skin, then realized what he was doing and shook her head. "How do you do that?"

"What?"

"Get me going. All right, I confess, I do object to your management style. It's too overbearing."

"Everybody knows where they stand with me. There aren't any surprises."

"A 'me Tarzan' sort of thing?"

"If it works."

The night closed around them, shutting off the rest of the office. They were, he realized, a man and a woman alone. The reason they were together seemed unimportant. He didn't care what they talked about, even if they argued. He only wanted to watch her try and convince him she knew best. The way she moved her hands as she spoke, the unconscious elegance, the slight tilting of her head, all intrigued him. She wore her beauty casually, as if she didn't quite believe it existed.

There hadn't been many women like her in his life. There hadn't been any. All his bed-buddies had wanted was to take from him. It was his fault, he acknowledged. He'd been the one who asked them out. But it had been easier to give away weekends in Paris and expensive jewelry than to let them inside him.

Lauren was the first woman he'd been attracted to who didn't want anything except to do her job. She challenged him mentally—he glanced at her mouth—and in other ways.

"Haven't you heard the old expression about honey catching more flies than vinegar?" she asked.

"I never believed it. Besides, I'm not interested in flies."

She leaned forward and rested her hands on the desk. Long, unpolished nails tapped on the wood surface. "You have no concept of patience or planning for the long haul."

"I'll plead guilty to the first charge. If I want something, I go after it."

She swallowed. "On your terms."

"Of course."

"And what if the object you're pursuing doesn't want to be caught?"

She ducked her head as she spoke. The light gleamed on the mahogany hair. It took every ounce of willpower not to ask her to take it down. He could almost see her delicate fingers slowly pulling out pins. One by one they would fall on the desk, clicking softly as they hit the wood. A strand at a time would tumble around her shoulders. Her eyes would widen and darken with desire as she began to unbutton—

He straightened in his chair. "Everything's gotta go sometime. It might as well be to me. We are talking about Tonikita Corporation here, aren't we?"

"What else?" But she avoided his gaze.

"Speaking of your Japanese friends, did you read the letter I sent over?"

"I don't think so."

"Sally should have brought you a copy this afternoon. I faxed it to them."

Lauren reached for a folder on her left. "She left these for me before she went home. I didn't get a chance to look at them." She opened the folder, then smiled at him. "Let me guess. It explains all the advantages of working with Baldwin International, details your past exploits, and warns them their days are numbered."

He leaned forward. "I can see I'm going to have to teach you to be more respectful."

She folded her hands in a show of mock submission. "I thought you *liked* input from your staff."

"Not when it's something I don't want to hear."

"Oh, sure. Isn't that the price you pay for an open-door policy?"

"Never." He laughed. "They always end up thinking just like me."

She shook her head. "I don't think you're going to be able to turn me into a replica of yourself. I'm not ready to give up the peace and serenity of the East to play cowboy."

The night played tricks on him. The quiet and darkness made him want to forget where they were and why they had met in the first place. Her voice—more sultry now, slow and sweet, liquid enough to drown in—made him want to mate with her. Like a predator, he felt the primal urge to take the tempting she-wolf, claim her, mark her, satisfy her and himself in a night of tension and torment, sweat and seduction. His hands closed into fists.

"So you think you're going to turn me into a spokesperson for Eastern culture?" he asked.

"No. You're going to do that all on your own."

The tension in the room affected her, despite her attempts to ignore the building electricity. She sat up straighter; deep breaths thrust her breasts higher. Soft silk molded their rounded shape.

Their eyes locked. Her expression softened as temptation quickly followed on the heels of confusion. She felt it now; there was no escape, no return. They'd reached the edge. Her hand holding the folder trembled slightly, and the light caught the gold and black of the company logo. The sight of the familiar lettering caught him like a blow to the belly.

My God, what was he thinking? If he planned to pull off this deal, he had to keep his mind on his business and his dick in his pants.

He forced his hands to relax. "Are you going to read the letter?"

Lauren blinked slowly, then cleared her throat. After slipping on her glasses, she sorted through the papers and found the one in question. When she looked back at him, it was as if the moment had never happened. The sultry vixen had been replaced by a highly qualified, coolly competent business associate.

She scanned the sheet. A furrow appeared between her brows. She reached the bottom and read it again.

"You promised." She spoke calmly, without a hint of accusation. At first he thought she was kidding.

"What specifically?"

"You promised that I would be just another employee, and that you wouldn't use my relationship with Yamashita to your personal advantage."

"Yes, but we also agreed that he would know you were on the team."

"Not like this." She tossed the letter toward him.

"What bothers you?"

"All of it." She rubbed the bridge of her nose. "I'm the topic of the letter. I suppose you think the paragraph where you explain that I have been hired specifically to custom-design an Eastern approach to the potential merger is subtle? And the place you remind him of my excellent work record with his company, well, that must be your way of establishing communication." She shook her head. "You're using me."

"That's not fair."

"It's the truth."

Jack leaned forward. He could take her anger. A good brawl between friends or co-workers never hurt anyone and often cleared the air. But this conversation made him uncomfortable. Although she was careful to conceal her feelings, he sensed her disappointment.

"You're taking this too personally," he said.

"And you're taking advantage."

"It's not like that. I hired you for two reasons, Lauren. One, because you're good at your job. And two, because of your past relationship with Yamashita. I didn't hide anything when we talked before."

"So in your mind this is a simple letter of introduction and not using my relationship with his family? Talk about shooting from the hip."

She was careful to keep her emotions concealed, but he found himself shifting in the chair. "Did you plan to be invisible? He would have figured it out during the negotiations."

"Yamashita has no reason to attend initial meetings,

and you know it. This is just semantics, Jack, just like . . . before.''

She'd almost said "the kiss," but caught herself in time. What a mess, Lauren thought. For a short time, she'd allowed herself to believe she could make a difference. It had been less than seventy-two hours and already he wasn't listening. He wanted her for her name and her connections. Everything else was just window dressing. Jack was controlling this show, start to finish. She'd been a fool.

She inhaled deeply. The letter was gone, and no amount of anger or disappointment was going to bring it back. She could salvage the situation, or she could walk away.

"I hate to see you upset," he said.

"I'm not."

She could see he knew she lied. But they both pretended. At least she had the professional satisfaction of knowing she hadn't actually given her feelings away. There had been no outburst, no tantrums. No tears.

"Then let me buy you dinner."

"I don't think so. It wouldn't be wise."

"Why?"

She forced herself to smile brightly and prayed it was enough. "This is business, Jack. And only business. Let's not make it something it's not."

He stared at her. For a second she thought he'd taken the rejection personally, but she dismissed the thought. If the gossip she'd heard was even half-true, he had enough lady friends to form a fan club.

"You're right," he said as he gathered up his coat and rose. "I didn't purposely mislead you."

"I know that. But even if you did just hire me for my connections, you're stuck with me. And like it or not, I'm going to do my job. Despite your Western style, I'm going to make damn sure you get that contract.''

He frowned. ''I believe in you, Lauren. You don't have to prove anything to me.''

''Maybe not. But I have something to prove to myself.''

FIVE

"No, Jack. Try it like this. Not so fast." Lauren demonstrated the movement. "Strong, but not rushed." She placed her hand on his back and urged him down. "Try it again. But go farther this time. Deeper. Really feel it in your thighs. The key is control."

He tilted his head and glanced at her out of the corner of his eyes. "So it's like making love?"

She shook her head, refusing to be suckered into yet another of his teasingly sensual conversations. "It's nothing like making love. It's much more like the tea ceremony. Now go all the way. I want to see a perfect forty-five-degree bow."

He straightened, then placing his hands on his thighs, leaned forward until his upper body was parallel with the floor. After holding the pose for precisely one and a half seconds, he returned to an upright position.

"How was that?"

She leaned against the wall and applauded. "Perfect."

"Good." He rotated his shoulders. "I have just one question."

"Yes?"

"What am I supposed to do with my tie?" He waved the offending garment. "It flaps when I bow, and looks very undignified."

"Use a tie tack."

"Not my style."

"Then get used to the flapping. You're the one who insisted on this particular etiquette lesson. I told you, Westerners aren't expected to bow. A simple tilt of the head is more than enough. Think of it as gift giving. It's the thought that counts."

Jack perched on the corner of her desk. The morning had been cloudy, but now rays of sunlight poked through her window. The view from her office included the lake and part of the skyline, but with her boss in the room, she had trouble seeing anything but him. Now that the lesson was over, she could go sit down. But all the chairs were close to him. Too close. Better to stand and be safe. She'd been officially employed by Baldwin International for two weeks. She'd been teaching the negotiation team the fine points of Japanese culture, had overseen countless projections and reports, and sat in on several strategy meetings. Fitting in with the team wasn't her problem. It was Jack. No, it was her and the way she reacted to Jack.

"I don't know about you," he said, rolling up his left sleeve to just below the elbow, "but I never liked that old saying. I remember being ten years old and not getting a bike for Christmas. My dad got me some science kit. I'm sure it was expensive, and he'd expected me to like it, but . . ." He shrugged.

"It wasn't a bike."

"No. My mom tried to tell me it was the thought that counted." He rolled up his other sleeve and grinned. "I didn't believe her."

"Did you ever tell your father?"

"No." The smile faded and he stared past her as if seeing memories she couldn't share. "That spring I started doing odd jobs around the neighborhood, mowing lawns, planting gardens, and I earned enough to buy it myself."

"So you decided what you wanted and went after it?"

"I learned early to depend on myself." Blue-gray eyes met her own. "I guess that hasn't changed."

"Obviously not."

"It's been two weeks, Lauren. Come on, aren't you the least bit willing to bend and admit I might actually be doing something right with my—what was it you said?—my aggressive Western management style?"

She glanced at the four-color charts gracing her walls and the stacks of reports generated by his research team. There wasn't any aspect of the potential joint venture that hadn't been discussed, plotted, analyzed fifteen different ways, and worked into a computer model.

"I'll admit your staff is efficient."

"And that they like their jobs?" The right side of his mouth tilted up just enough to expose his dimple.

"They seem to."

"But?"

"But you could use a little balance here. You don't have to be number one to be successful."

"Bullshit."

She blinked. "Excuse me?"

"Are you telling me you'll be happy with anything less than a signed contract?"

She risked getting closer to him and sank into the leather chair in front of her desk. "No, but that's not what we're talking about. In life—"

He cut her off with a laugh. "In *anything* there is only winning. Second place doesn't count."

"So you fire everyone who isn't first? Must make for a streamlined payroll."

"You're exaggerating."

"I'm taking your idea to its logical conclusion. Based on only caring about the best, there can only be one that matters. So if the top salesperson earns a million five in sales and the second best does a million four, you discredit her."

"Or him." He folded his arms over his chest. "That's not what I meant and you know it. I'm talking about an overall philosophy."

"Success at any price?"

He frowned. "Why do I know I'm going to get into trouble no matter what I answer?"

She smiled. "Because it's true. If you say yes, you come off as a heartless raider. If you say no, you're a wimp."

He nodded. "Then I take the fifth."

"Coward."

"I prefer to think of it as a strategic retreat."

"I wouldn't have thought 'retreat' was part of your vocabulary."

"Despite rumors to the contrary, I *can* be flexible."

"If it suits you."

He looked surprised. "Why else?"

"Oh, Jack, what am I going to do with you?"

His mobile mouth, with its potentially lethal grin,

straightened. A gleam flickered in his smoky irises. Instantly he radiated raw masculine power and desire.

Oh no, she thought, straightening in the chair. Despite her sensible business suit and conservative shoes, despite the hours she'd spent sternly talking to herself about the merits of a purely professional relationship, he got to her. On some primal level, they clicked. She didn't know if it was subconscious signals or scent or souls that recognized their mates from a previous life. Whatever, it was potent and dangerous. He only had to look, or smile, and she was ready to be taken. The attraction would have been awkward on any job, but here, now, it was especially unwelcome. She had something to prove. She'd been hired to do a job, and come hell or high water, or bone-melting attraction, she was going to get it done. To borrow from the man in question, this was one victory she'd pay any price to claim.

"What I meant," she said hastily, "was that here everything is measured by performance rather than attitude. In many companies in Japan, employees are evaluated on dedication to the company and the ability to get along with co-workers, rather than innovation or self-motivation."

He grimaced. "So you could have some jerk who's incompetent, but he'd be kept on because everyone likes him?"

"You're not listening. Of course, an employee unable to do the job would be removed from that position, but if he was truly doing the best he could, he wouldn't be fired. The company made a commitment to him when he was hired, and he in turn will give his all to the company. They'll find him another position."

"That's crazy. What if he's a complete loser?"

She smiled sweetly. Okay, sometimes it felt good to

be the predator, she thought as she zeroed in for the kill. "As the manager who hired him, it would be your error for choosing him in the first place, not his for being unable to measure up."

He opened his mouth to respond, then closed it. "Interesting concept."

She grinned and said nothing.

"You think you won that one, don't you?" He rose and walked behind her desk to the window. "Damn, I think your view is better than mine. How did that happen?"

After crossing her legs, she slipped one pump off her foot and let it dangle on her toes. Silence.

He planted his hands on his hips. "I give. You get that point."

He spoke without turning around. Sunlight silhouetted his body. From shoulders to hips, his shape followed a perfect inverted triangle. She could almost see the muscles rippling under the pale blue shirt. Her throat grew dry.

"How does that translate into what we're going to be doing with Tonikita Corporation?" he asked without turning around.

"There are a couple of people who don't fit in. I'd like to discuss taking them off the team."

"Who?"

"Wilson and Johnson."

"Why?"

"Wilson is too inexperienced. She speaks at the wrong time and blurts out answers without thinking. When I tried to talk about it, she brushed me off. I think she's so terrified of failing, she can't think straight. Give her a chance on something smaller."

He glanced at her over his shoulder. "In other words,

the manager who hired her is responsible for her position in the company, and he should make it right for her."

"I couldn't have said it better myself." She bit her lip to keep from smiling.

"And Johnson?"

There was something in the way he asked the question. Lauren inhaled sharply. Looked like she was about to tread on some toes.

"He has contempt for all things Japanese."

Jack turned slowly until he was facing her. Strong arms folded over his chest. She didn't need a Ph.D. to read *his* body language.

"And?" he asked quietly.

"He makes you look like a Tokyo native. His attitude stinks, and it shows."

"He's my best player."

"Maybe in the past, but not this time." She uncrossed her legs and leaned forward. "He swaggers without even walking. He's not interested in being on the team, he wants to be the star."

"He's giving you trouble in the training sessions, isn't he?"

She shrugged. "This isn't personal."

"I never thought it was."

"There's a German contract coming up."

One dark brow raised. "How did you hear that?"

She dismissed the question with a wave of her hand. "I hear everything. Let him handle that. They'll appreciate the machismo more. Give him an arena in which he can win."

Jack sighed. "I'm training him for the executive floor."

"I guessed."

"How?"

"Maybe it was the slight resemblance to someone in this room."

"We don't look anything alike."

"That's not what I meant and you know it." She leaned back. "I'm serious about this, Jack."

"Yeah."

She held her breath. It was their first official disagreement. He wanted Johnson on the team. That had been obvious from the moment he'd been introduced to her. She'd tried to make it work, but it took effort on both parts. She couldn't even say she didn't like the young upstart. There was too much of Jack in his manner not to.

Jack sat in the chair behind her desk. "All right, he's off the project." He held up a hand to stop her. "Don't say it. I won't punish him. The manager is responsible and all that. You don't have to tell me twice."

"I don't want you to think—"

"Lauren, it's okay. I respect your judgment. I told you before, this is your project. I want this contract, and I'm willing to do whatever it takes. Are there any other problems with the team?"

"None."

"Good. What's next on the agenda?"

Before she could answer, there was a light tap on her door.

"Come in," she called.

"I brought those letters and—" Sally stepped into the room and glanced from Jack sitting behind the desk to Lauren sitting in front. "Has there been some change you want to tell me about?"

Lauren chuckled. "No, this is still my office, but he

can't bear to see a desk without wanting to sit behind it.''

"Oh really.'' Sally handed her the papers. "I'm not sure that's true. I never see him trying to sit behind a secretary's desk.''

"Hmm. There is that whole issue of power." Lauren signed the sheets, then glanced at Jack. He glared back.

"I'm in the room, you know,'' he said. "It's not polite to speak as if I'm not.''

"Sensitive," Sally said.

Lauren smiled sympathetically. "I've found that with the entire gender. Their feelings are hurt so easily. And they're *so* emotional.''

Jack growled.

Sally took the signed letters and winked at him. "You love the attention.''

"Get back to work.''

She crossed the room and paused by the door. "Need anything else, Lauren?''

"I'd appreciate it if those could go out in today's mail.''

"Not a problem.'' She closed the door softly behind her.

Jack glanced at the clock, then loosened his tie. "How long have you hated men?''

Lauren grinned. " 'Hate' is such a strong word.''

"Had contempt for, then.''

"We were teasing.''

"I know. What were we talking about?''

He pulled the short end of the tie out of the knot, then tugged it free from under his collar. She watched the unstudied movements. The masculine grace held her mesmerized. Strong fingers unbuttoned first one, then the second button on his pale shirt. The slight vee exposed tanned skin and one or two crinkly black hairs. Somewhere in the pit of her stomach, butterflies joined hands and soft-shoed in time with the alarm buzzing in her brain. She cleared her throat.

"You wanted to know what was next on the agenda, I believe." She practically sighed in relief. Her voice sounded normal. He couldn't possibly know what he did to her. She could keep on believing that as long as she ignored the gleam in his eyes.

"That'll keep," he said, tilting his head back against the chair. "Tell me what you think of all this."

"All what?"

"The project. It's been two weeks. Are we on track? Last time we talked, you objected strongly to my procedures."

"Among other things." She wanted to call back the words and bite down hard on her tongue to keep herself from saying them, but it was too late.

"I don't regret sending the letter." He stared at her for several seconds. "I do regret your feelings on the matter. I didn't set out to hurt you or make you feel used. For what it's worth, I would have hired you even without your connection to Yamashita."

She'd been wondering, but hadn't known how to ask the question, or if she would have believed the answer. She still wasn't sure she did, but it was nice to be told.

This was the danger, she thought as she crossed her legs and let her pump dangle again. Not the sexual attraction. She was an adult; that was easily handled. No, the real threat lay in his take-charge attitude. She wasn't worried about being overwhelmed exactly, it was more that she was vulnerable to a long-term siege. All that energy and attention he focused on business. Dear God, if he ever sent a tenth of it her way, she'd be gone for sure. If he'd been a complete jerk, she'd be immune, but no, he had to have occasional flashes of being a nice guy. It wasn't fair!

"Thanks for telling me that," she said.

His gaze narrowed. "You sound as if you don't believe me."

"I didn't say that."

"You didn't have to."

"I appreciate the compliment."

He looked unconvinced.

"Really," she added.

"Lauren." Her name came out as a growl.

"Jack, I think . . . ." She paused, then smiled slowly. "Maybe it's my turn to take the fifth."

She held her breath as he studied her. For a second she thought he was going to push her to tell him why she doubted his word. And she couldn't do that. There were too many things mixed up in her head. The need to be successful on the job battled with her attraction to her boss.

His gaze traveled from her eyes to her mouth, then down her body, pausing on her crossed leg and the pump dangling on her toes. A muscle clenched in his jaw. His body visibly tightened.

He exhaled abruptly and turned to glance at the wall on his right. "I see you put up all your awards and diplomas. I thought you believed in impressing people with substance."

Thank you, she breathed silently. He wasn't going to push her. Yet. She knew the reprieve was temporary. "I wanted to fit in. It seemed to be important to you."

"Another insult?"

"Not at all."

He leaned back in her chair. "Sure, Lauren." He

pointed to the wall. "Why Tokyo University? I thought most military brats came home for college."

"They do." She shrugged. "I'd been accepted to a couple of schools here, but I thought I'd do better with a Japanese degree. I wanted to work on the language. There are subtle nuances that can take a non-native years to understand. Besides, with two older brothers and a father who's a general, I was ready to be on my own." It had been her mother's idea, she remembered. Ellen Reese had wanted to give her only daughter an arena of her own in which to succeed.

"But you came back to the States right after college and went to work for the Language Institute," Jack said. "Wouldn't it have made more sense to stay there and work for a couple of years?"

She shifted in her chair, fighting the need to be defensive. "I thought we'd already gone through the interview process."

He raised one eyebrow. "I'm just curious about you and your past. Is that a problem?"

"Of course not." She was overreacting.

"Did you have job offers in Japan?"

"A couple. I hadn't really done a lot of interviews. There were openings. An American who speaks fluent Japanese and knows her way around both cultures wouldn't have too much trouble finding a job."

"But you didn't stay. Why?"

If she closed her eyes, she'd be able to remember the overpowering scent of cherry blossoms and the look in Jiro's eyes. *The bottom line, kid, is that it won't work.* His words echoed again and again. It had been months before she'd been able to wake up in the morning without hearing them rattling around the room. With the passage of time, she'd had the hindsight to wonder if she suffered more from being taken advantage of than because her heart had been broken irreparably. But she'd never forgotten.

"A lot of reasons," she said calmly.

"Such as?"

"None of the jobs really appealed to me. I missed my family. I missed real hamburgers. What else?" She paused, not sure how much of the truth to tell. "I suppose I realized that I'd never truly fit in. I'd always be different—in both body and soul."

Those blue-gray eyes flickered back to her face. She felt the probing glance, did her best to keep the pain hidden, but it was a futile attempt.

"Someone broke your heart," he said softly.

He was the best, she acknowledged. Probing his opponents, finding their weaknesses, and going for the kill is what Jack did better than anyone. So she shouldn't be surprised he had quickly grasped the source of her pain. But she was. What else would he be able to figure out?

She dismissed his concern with a shake of her head. "It was a long time ago."

"Was it?"

The simple question required only a yes or no answer. But he wasn't asking about the passage of days or months or years. He was asking about the depth of the pain, if she still remembered, if she'd been damaged past reaching.

"A very long time ago," she said. "We were kids."

"Another woman?"

A very close friend, she thought bitterly. "More like another culture, I think," she said. It was part of the truth, at least. "He wanted a traditional Japanese wife."

"Knowing what went wrong doesn't always make the hurt easier to get over."

His intensity made her uncomfortable. Quiet had settled in the office as the day faded into late afternoon. Although they weren't alone on the floor, she felt isolated. It was dangerous because Jack was dangerous. He made her think about wanting, and being alive again. He made her hungry in a way that was new and frighteningly powerful. She'd seen too many women make fools of themselves over a man and had never understood the driving force.

Until now.

Those ever-changing eyes took in her features, and the look was as tangible as a touch. When he toyed with a pen from her desk—rubbing his thumb and index finger over the smooth metal, sliding it back and forth against his palm—her skin heated as though she were being caressed. It would be simple to be a fool for Jack. The only problem was, she couldn't afford the cost of losing.

More than her job was on the line. Some fragile center of self-confidence had been damaged many years before. She was just beginning to find her way back. If she gave in to what he silently offered, she'd lose it all.

"Lauren, I don't want you to think that I usually react this way to a colleague of mine," he said, staring directly at her.

She opened her mouth to answer, then closed it. Had he read her mind?

"What way?" she managed at last. When had it gotten so easy to lie?

"Don't.'

He rose to his feet and came around the desk. She

fought the urge to shrink back in her seat. He paused in front of her, looming large and powerful. And masculine.

Bracing his hands on the arms of her chair, he squatted down. The vee of his thighs trapped her; her knees nestled inches from his crotch. Heat enveloped and surrounded her.

"When this is over," he said quietly, "I will come for you. I don't care about schedules or plans. You will be mine."

"No."

He smiled. "You deny it?"

She squared her shoulders. "With every breath I take."

"Ah, Lauren, you want me. It's in your eyes. And I want you. It would be . . ."

He raised his hand to touch her hair. She remained perfectly still. One finger tucked a stray curl behind her ear. The contact split through her like lightning through a sapling. Need rippled through her belly and inflamed her thighs.

"Perfect," he murmured. "You know it and I know it. What's the problem?"

"This is business."

"For now."

She shook her head. "I won't play second fiddle to your real life."

"I'm not asking you to *play* at all. It would be very, very real."

For how long? She didn't voice the question; there was no point. She already knew the answer. He found her attractive. She intrigued him. But intrigue wasn't enough to build a relationship on. If she got him the contract, he'd want to exercise his bonus option. And that bonus option was her.

He would take her body and pleasure it. She didn't doubt that. Just listening to his voice, watching him watch her, convinced her that Jack Baldwin knew how to please a woman. As she feared, the intensity of his personality could be daunting. And seductive. As long as she stayed out of dark corners and empty apartments, namely his, she'd be safe.

It sounded simple, she thought as he rose to his feet. But as surely as she believed in white sales in January, she knew that if he touched her once, kissed her as he had that afternoon at her house, she would be little more than aching putty in his hands.

"Don't ignore the fact that—" He quickly looked away, as if he'd changed his mind about something.

"Don't ignore what?"

He pinned her with his gaze. "That we might actually need each other."

"What?" She couldn't have heard him correctly.

"Don't think I'm going to let you walk away from this," he said. "There isn't any—"

A knock at the door cut him off.

"Come in," Lauren called, because there wasn't any choice. *Need.* Had he said *need?*

Sally opened the door and stepped inside. "It just came over the fax," she said, waving a sheet of paper in the air.

Lauren stood as desire and her questions were quickly replaced by apprehension. She wanted the chance to prove herself, she thought. So why was she suddenly terrified that Baldwin International was about to be invited to bid on the contract?

Fear of failure and fear of success, she told herself grimly. Interesting dilemma.

Jack leaned against her desk and crossed his ankles. "What do they say?"

If she didn't know better, she'd think he didn't really care about the message. Not to mention the fact that there wasn't even a hint that thirty seconds before, he'd been doing his damnedest to convince her that seduction was inevitable.

"We're in."

He smiled. "Good. When?"

Sally glanced at the fax. "Three weeks from yesterday."

"That's not much time." Jack took the sheet and scanned it quickly. "Can you be ready?" he asked Lauren.

"Of course."

He nodded. "I have some calls to make. I'll need to reschedule some appointments to be available."

Lauren moved aside to let him pass. He took a step, then paused.

"We've begun," he said. "It's just a matter of time."

"Until the win?" she asked.

One eyebrow raised. "That's an interesting way to think about it. I like it. Yes, Lauren. Until the win. And I will win."

He walked out quickly. Sally said something about making copies of the fax and followed on his heels.

She was a fool to let him get to her, Lauren thought as she pressed her hands to her flushed cheeks. Casual relationships had never been her style. She had the broken heart to prove it. But Jack wouldn't understand anything else. She sighed. At least they had the deal.

*   *   *

Jack hurried toward the conference room. He glanced at his watch and swore. Crosstown traffic and a lunch that had been both long and boring had conspired to make him late.

As he pushed open the left of the double doors, he heard Lauren's pleasant low voice speaking to the assembled group.

"The key to this sort of negotiation is to remember the purpose. We aren't going to get a signed deal with Tonikita Corporation. The correct term for what we're doing is *nemawashi*."

"She's got to be kidding," Jack muttered as he slipped into the room and leaned against the rear wall. Twenty of his employees sat behind long desks. Most were busy taking notes. "There better not be a spelling test on that."

Lauren wrote out the word on the wide white board in the front of the room. Her felt pen moved silently as she formed the letters. Even her handwriting told a story about her, he thought as he folded his arms over his chest. Strong, but not overly large, full of character, yet easy to read. Just like the lady herself.

"*Nemawashi*," she repeated.

The class spoke after her.

Jack groaned softly. He'd put in a late night preparing for the business lunch he'd attended. The little sleep he had managed had been haunted by a leggy redhead with breasts a man would sell his soul to touch. And taste.

His mouth watered and he swallowed.

Lauren glanced up and caught him in the act. As she smiled, he thanked God that she couldn't read his mind.

"The translation of the word is 'the binding up of

the roots of a tree prior to its being transplanted.' ''
She smiled.

It was directed at the class in general, he told himself. Not anyone in particular. Yet he found himself smiling in return, as if she'd meant it for him alone.

"The loose meaning of that is a preliminary and informal sounding out of people's ideas. We're meeting with Tonikita Corporation to find out if the two companies are compatible, not to close the deal. If you rush forward half-cocked, you'll blow it."

Unlike the smile, he didn't have to guess who *that* comment was meant for. It had his name written all over it. He pushed off the wall and started up the center aisle of the meeting room.

"Why don't we take a ten-minute break," she said, glancing at him. Her expression was innocence itself, but he knew better.

"Sure," he said, stopping at her side. "Clear out the troops so they don't witness the conflagration?"

"Are we going to fight?" Bright green eyes danced with humor.

"Don't tempt me."

Most of her lipstick had worn away, but enough remained to add a shine to her mouth. The corners of her lips turned up slightly.

"How was your meeting?" she asked.

"Long and boring. What did I miss here?"

"Oh, you meant you were going to be here at one o'clock *today*." She made a great show of checking her watch. "I thought you meant another Wednesday. Perhaps a different week or month."

"Okay, yeah, I'm late. I apologize. So what did I miss?"

Sally came up and joined them. She fluttered her

lashes. "A discussion on the importance of silence. You'd have loved it."

Jack stared at Lauren. "She's kidding."

"Nope."

"Silence?"

"Uh-huh."

"As in not speaking?"

"The same."

He sighed. "Great. Fill me in."

Sally shook her head. "I'd love to hear this, but I have some calls to return." She patted Lauren's back. "Good luck."

"So," he said. "Silence."

"It is considered wise in Japanese business practice to pause and think before answering a question," she said. "It shows you're not jumping in with a foolish remark or suggestion."

He pulled out the chair behind a desk in the first row and sank into the leather seat. "Kind of puts a damper on brainstorming."

"Agreed. But that's not the purpose of the meeting, is it? It's not so much for your team as for Tonikita's, although it wouldn't be a bad idea to wait before answering. However, the Tonikita people will expect to be given as much time as necessary to formulate their answers. If you rush them, you'll ruin everything."

"Wait a minute." He held up one hand. "When you say 'you,' do you mean 'you' in general, as in all the people in this room, or 'you' as in me specifically?"

She moved behind the lectern and straightened her notes. Twice. Silence and not speaking, huh? She was sure getting her message across loud and clear.

"I see," he said at last. "You're telling me this lesson wasn't for the team at large."

"You do have a habit of barreling in."

"Agreed."

"You don't have to be so proud of it." She placed her forearms on the lectern and leaned forward, toward him. "Trust me."

"With my life. Actually with my company, which is worth more."

"I wish that were true."

He grinned. "It is. The company is worth several million, while my personal value, if sold for replacement parts, is substantially less."

She moved to the side table to pick up a glass of water, but didn't smile back. "That's not what I meant."

"I know."

He slumped down in the seat and placed his elbows on the armrests. Steepling his hands, he rested his chin on the tips of his middle fingers.

"I can only promise to try," he said at last. "You should consider that you want more than trust. You want control."

"And that's a problem?"

It was all he had, he thought. It had never let him down. When he hadn't gotten the bike he'd wanted when he was ten he'd earned his own. When he'd been sent to boarding school and his father hadn't bothered to bring him home for the holidays, he'd made plans with other kids so that it wouldn't hurt so bad. When his bed-buddies got too close to finding out the truth, he sent them on their way with a fond farewell and a sparkling piece of jewelry. Without his control, he'd be nowhere, and no one.

"I know in my head you're telling me the truth, but

in my gut . . ." He shrugged. "It's never lied to me before."

"It's not lying," she said. "It's misinformed. You work from instinct, but you have no point of reference this time. Everything you believe to be true is useless. Worse, it's going to hurt the deal. I'm not playing games, Jack. This isn't about ego or power. It's about being successful."

She wore her hair long today. The mahogany tresses tumbled over her shoulders and down her back. Her dress should have been unattractive as hell. The dull moss green fabric fell in a straight line from her shoulders to just above the knees. Gold buttons marched up the front. No pin or splash of color relieved the severe lines. Yet her breasts and hips pressed against the cloth, hinting at the womanly shape concealed beneath. Calves curved and narrowed into trim ankles and small feet tucked into sexy snakeskin pumps. Instead of thinking of the schoolmarm from his worst nightmare, he found himself wondering if the buttons in front unfastened, and what she wore under them.

"So what's the solution?" he asked.

"I already told you. Stop playing at these sessions. Listen and learn."

He glanced away. Okay, she was right. He knew she was the perfect person for the job. He *could* give her a break. Give her the ball and let her run with it. If they got the contract, it would be because of her, anyway. But he wasn't convinced that the Tonikita team couldn't handle a little straight talk. Diplomacy was one thing, Eastern philosophy another. Although he'd pay quite a bit to see Lauren in a sweat about something.

"Uh-oh." She sipped from her glass. "I don't like that look. What are you thinking?"

"I was wondering if you ever sweat."

"You're kidding. You want to see me sweat?"

"Among other things, Godzilla-eyes."

Color flared on her cheeks. "Jack."

"Sorry."

But he wasn't. He liked knowing he got to her. They were four weeks into their arrangement, but he still hadn't gotten her out of his system. Still, he was willing to wait. With Lauren, that was turning out to be pleasurable in its own right. Sex was easy. Wondering, imagining; he hadn't known they could be fun, too. He'd taken more cold showers in the last month than he had since he turned eighteen and had a crush on a cheerleader in his college economics class. The crush had ended the second time they'd gone all the way in the back of his Mustang.

When he'd gotten Tonikita to sign, he was going to give in to the fantasies. Then he'd be able to walk away. That had always been his solution to relationships. Keep 'em happy, then get 'em out.

He ignored the voice that whispered that this time might be different, because Lauren was different. She wasn't impressed with him or his power. Interesting to find out he liked that in a woman. Every day she surprised him; every day he liked her more. Still, when he'd won the contract, he'd move on to another challenge, and she'd write her own ticket in the international market.

But there was still a little matter of seeing her sweat.

"You play racquetball?" he asked.

She sipped from her glass, then set it back on the table. "I've played *at* it. I think there's a difference."

"Want to try it?"

"With you?"

"Sure. Unless you're chicken?"

She folded her arms and glared down at him. "Afraid of you? Be serious."

"Great. Tomorrow. My club." He reached for a pen and jotted down the address. "Six."

"A.M.?"

"Best time of the day." He winked. "Male energy is at its peak."

SIX

Lauren's shoes squeaked on the highly waxed wooden floor. The white walls, marked only by the occasional shoe scuffs and round circles from hit balls, reflected the overhead light with almost blinding intensity.

The racquetball court was completely enclosed. And, thank God, the sides were solidly constructed. The receptionist had offered a court with a glass back, but Lauren didn't feel the need to let the world witness her potential humiliation, and had taken one that was private.

She paced back and forth, trying to burn off the nervous energy that had kept her tossing and turning most of the night. It was just a game, she told herself firmly. A sport. There was no social significance to playing racquetball with one's boss. No rules were being broken, no line would be crossed.

Uh-huh, she thought as she pulled at the hem of her suddenly too short shorts. If she believed that, maybe it was time to go beach-property-shopping in Arizona.

She twirled the racquet in her hands. This was a nonwork activity. Their first. It wasn't even disguised as "a working dinner to discuss the client." They were here to have fun. At least that's what she thought. Jack's comment about wanting to see her sweat hadn't made any sense at all.

The handle of the heavy door clicked down suddenly. She spun to face the entrance.

Jack stepped into the room, a racquet in one hand, an unopened can of balls in the other. She drew in a breath and managed a shaky greeting, all the while trying not to stare.

"Good morning," he said.

"Morning," she mumbled.

His clothes didn't shock her. Rather, the lack of them definitely had the potential to mess with her concentration. Nervously she glanced at the floor, only to find her gaze irresistibly drawn back up his body.

Athletic shoes and heavy white socks led into long, long legs. It was May in Chicago, for heaven's sake, but his exposed skin had been tanned a honeyed brown. Thigh muscles rippled with each movement. Red nylon shorts sat loosely on narrow hips. For a second she wondered what he wore under the thin fabric, then shied away from the vivid image her mind presented of a man—this man—wearing nothing at all.

From the waistband of his shorts, several inches of hard washboard stomach bisected by a dark shaft of hair filled the area below his cropped Ivy League T-shirt. The shoulders, she was used to, she thought as she briefly took in their breadth. Her appraisal stopped just short of his eyes. She couldn't bear to see his amusement.

The loud popping of the can being opened startled her. She jumped back.

"Ready?" Jack asked.

"Sure. You want to serve?"

"Let's warm up first. Did you stretch?"

She nodded and tugged again at the hem of her shorts.

"I haven't," he said, setting the racquet on the floor and slipping three balls into one pocket.

She glanced away, but in the narrow two-story room, there wasn't much to look at except Jack. He pressed his palms flat against one wall and took a step backwards to stretch out his calf. Powerful muscles bunched and released at the movement. The racquetballs in his pocket pulled the thin nylon taut across his buttocks, outlining the high, rounded flesh.

She'd never been much of a morning person, preferring to wake up slowly and move at her own pace. Certainly she'd never been interested in making love before noon. Yet as Jack shifted his weight, stepping back with the opposite leg and stretching, sexual heat roared to life inside her belly and raced out all along her body. On her arms and back, tiny goose bumps erupted, sensitizing her skin. Her breasts swelled against the cotton of her athletic bra. And between her legs a sudden dampness moistened her silk panties. He'd been in the room less than five minutes.

Lauren closed her eyes and took a deep, cleansing breath. As she concentrated on inhaling and exhaling, she cleared her mind and tried to picture a quiet stream. But instead of the peaceful pool, erotic images flashed through her mind.

"Hey!" Jack's voice pulled her out of her attempts to relax.

"What?"

"No Zen. This meeting is strictly Western."

He tossed her a ball and the megawatt grin. On cue, her hand closed over the ball, and her knees threatened to collapse.

Help me, she breathed silently to any force that would listen, and then served.

An hour later, she knew she'd been had. The lopsided score—she made one point for every eight or nine of his—proved that he was indeed a ringer.

"You didn't tell me you were about to turn pro," she said, dropping her racquet on the floor and bending over to catch her breath.

"I play occasionally," he admitted.

"Hourly?"

"Three or four times a week."

She groaned. "Let me guess. You and the other he-man types meet at six in the morning."

"Sometimes it's five."

She pressed her hands on her thighs and forced herself to stand upright. Her T-shirt clung to her in damp patches. Several strands of hair had escaped her ponytail. Heat and moisture plastered them to her neck. There wasn't a mirror, but she had a feeling she looked like she felt: flushed and winded and completely out of her league.

"Are we done yet?" she asked.

"I haven't reached twenty-one." He bounced a ball against the center of the racquet. "You have to win by two points."

"Somehow I don't think you should sweat it," she said wryly. "I have four points and you have, what, eighteen?"

"Seventeen."

"Oh, well, seventeen. Gee, that makes all the difference in the world. I can see why you're worried about finishing the game. Heaven knows what would happen to your reputation if I scored again." She picked up her racquet and stepped behind the line. "Go ahead and serve."

Jack chuckled and tossed her the ball. She caught it neatly. "You serve," he said.

"Thanks. That'll be a big help. Maybe I'll beat my previous record and score five whole points in one game."

"Shut up and serve."

She stuck out her tongue as she walked past him. He grinned. This had been one of his better ideas, he thought as he shifted his weight to the left and returned the ball. She hit the volley easily.

The back-and-forth play continued unbroken for several minutes. Jack stayed in the rear of the court, where he could both keep the ball in motion and watch Lauren. Despite her lack of experience at the game, she moved with a natural grace. Given a few lessons and a couple of months of serious play, she'd be a challenge to him on the court. And off, he thought as he caught a corner shot and returned it gently. He'd wanted to see her sweat, and like everything else, she did it well.

Moisture glistened on her face and down her neck. He lunged forward and hit the ball before it bounced. As he turned, he winked at her. She blushed slightly, then looked away. A bead of perspiration trickled down the front of her throat and disappeared into the damp cotton of her peach T-shirt. Her lips would taste salty.

"Look out," she called as she raced to meet a long shot. He sidestepped and she brushed past him.

They'd generate a lot of heat together, he acknowledged, fighting the urge to capture her in his arms. Too much. Lauren was the kind of woman looking for—

He frowned. He wasn't sure what, exactly. She struck him as the type of woman who wanted a commitment. Not his style at all. And a family. She'd be a great mother, he thought. Patient and fair. He could see her with a baby in her arms and two little ones playing nearby.

The ball bounced toward him. He lobbed it up. After it hit the floor, Lauren raced forward and tapped it. The ball bounced off the wall and landed about six inches into the court.

"Why, you little cheater!" Jack raced forward, but he was too late. The ball bounced on the floor a second time, then rolled toward him.

"Yes!" Lauren pumped her right arm in a sign of victory. "Another point. That makes five, and beats my previous record."

"Lucky shot," he complained.

"I don't care how I get them, as long as I do." She picked up a towel from the corner of the room and used it to wipe her face.

"You haven't won yet."

"And we both know I won't, but I'll take the little I can get and be content with that victory."

She threw down the towel. He stepped toward the center of the court and served the ball. "Maybe I should challenge Yamashita to a game instead of going through the whole negotiation process."

"Interesting concept. Kind of like the samurai fighting to determine control of the whole village."

Jack slammed the ball into the corner, easily taking

the point. "You mean I have an idea that you approve of?"

"It has merit. The only problem is that Yamashita isn't even in the country."

"When does he arrive? Negotiations start in less than three weeks."

She returned his serve and brushed her bangs out of her eyes. She wasn't wearing any makeup. He liked the creamy paleness of her skin and the way the freckles stood out on her nose and upper cheeks. During the workday, her makeup muted them until they blended away, but now he could count them. If she stood still that long and he was allowed that close.

"Yamashita won't be at the negotiations."

"What?" He let the ball bounce past him. "Are you kidding?"

"No. I've tried to tell you, their style is very different. The spokesperson is rarely the man in charge."

"Then how do we get anything done? I don't want to waste time on a group of flunkies."

"Jack." She moved closer and rested her hand on his forearm. As he'd thought before, the heat generated was enough to melt the varnish off the wooden floor. "The key decision maker won't bother to be present until he is convinced it is right for the two companies involved to reach agreement. By showing up initially, Yamashita would be sending the message that he is ready to close a deal."

"Isn't that what we're supposed to do?"

"I said 'close the deal.' At this point we're all going to discuss the value of initiating a deal at all."

"I don't like this. No company I've ever dealt with—"

"Has been Japanese," she interrupted. "I warned

you. Tonikita Corporation is very old school. They don't, to quote a friend from the South, truck with foreigners.''

He turned his arm and grabbed her hand. Both their palms were damp. Her warm skin slipped against his. She seemed on the verge of pulling back. Before she could, he laced his fingers with hers and held her in place.

The scent of her body drifted to him. She smelled clean and womanly. It was the kind of fragrance that would cling to his sheets and pillows and haunt him forever. Green eyes glanced everywhere but at his. He made her nervous. That much was obvious. Like everything she did, it pleased him.

Sweat darkened the baby-fine hairs at her temples and caused them to curl into ringlets. With his free hand, he touched her chin. Startled, she glanced up at him.

"What are you doing?" she asked softly. Her voice quivered slightly with the words. A deep breath raised her chest—her breasts—toward him. The damp cotton clung and outlined the feminine curves underneath.

"Counting freckles."

"What?"

"You have eleven on this cheek." He gently touched the silky smoothness. "And fourteen over here." He brushed the other side. "And on your nose—"

"Ten. I've been told. You shouldn't—"

But he never heard what he shouldn't do. Lowering his mouth to hers, he cut off the words, swallowing the sound and her shocked breath of air with his kiss. Both their racquets clattered to the floor.

Lips pressed against lips. She tasted of salty sweetness and shy surrender. With the barest flick of his tongue, she parted to admit him. He hesitated, outlining her mouth, dipping inside for brief forays, but refusing to plunge into her waiting moistness.

Hunger overwhelmed him. Need and desire and heat sucked the control from his body and threatened to tumble him into an abyss with all the subtlety of an avalanche. The urge to pull her close, to rip the clothes from their bodies, shook him with its intensity.

Their fingers remained entwined. To keep himself from reacting to the primal need to claim her, he ran his free hand down her arm until their palms touched and fingers laced. He pulled her arms behind his back and drew her closer. Bare legs brushed. Her hips and stomach cradled the hard proof of his intentions. Full breasts nestled against his chest.

His rational self reminded him that control must be maintained at all costs. She was not for him. Yet no woman had ever been able to test him, or push him past his self-prescribed limits. Until Lauren.

"Stop playing," she whispered, then pressed her mouth harder against his.

"I'm not."

"Yes, you are."

He was. They both knew it. Still he didn't respond, only allowed himself to trace endless circles on her lips, to nibble the corners, to suck gently.

"Kiss me, damn it!" she whispered.

She jerked her hands free and reached up to cup his head. Holding him still, she raised herself up on tiptoes and angled her lips over his. When he opened his mouth to protest, she plunged inside and mated with all the urgency of the passionate woman he knew her to be.

There was no time to think, no need to do anything but feel. Her tongue circled and stroked his. Her boldness excited him past the point of caution until there was nothing in the world but the sensation of their mouths and bodies.

With a groan of surrender, he wrapped his arms around her and pulled her tight against him. Slipping one hand down her spine, he cupped the curve of her buttocks and gently squeezed the pliant flesh. She moaned. The sound vibrated in her chest. With his other hand, he followed the lines of her ribs around to the front of her T-shirt. Her fingers twined in his hair, pulling him closer, urging him on.

As his palm slipped up to cup her breast, his tongue plunged past her lips and into her mouth, forcing her to retreat and be claimed. She rocked her hips against his erection. Now it was his turn to moan as the heat of her femininity brushed back and forth, then up and down along his hardened length. Pressure built. It would be so easy to free himself of his shorts and jockstrap. The thought of first the cool air, then her hot, damp palm caressing him, caused him to swell to the point of pain.

He needed to know she matched him flame for flame, hunger for hunger. While the hand on her derriere encouraged her to keep up the rocking motion, the fingers of the other discovered the curve of her breast. His thumb swept across the cotton T-shirt and sports bra beneath, searching for, then finding, the puckering of her hardening nipple. He flicked the sensitized tip once, twice, then pressed down in a gentle circling motion. Lauren responded with a caught breath followed by a sharp nip on his lower lip.

"You like that," he murmured.

"Jack."

He bent down and forced her head back. While trailing kisses down her neck, he moved his hand away from her breast and toward the waistband of her shorts. He slipped easily beneath the elastic band and under her panties.

"Don't," she said, without much conviction.

"You can feel me." He rubbed his hardness against her hip. "I want to know what I do to you."

"You already know." Her eyes remained closed.

His first two fingers plunged through the springy curls into the dampness below.

"So wet and hot. All for me." He breathed the words against her neck.

"Jack. I can't."

"Of course you can."

"No. It's— Oh!"

He found, then moved back and forth against, her sensitive core. She sagged against him. Breasts thrust forward, straining against the confining bra and shirt. He looked at her face. Her lips parted as if to draw in more air. Color flared on her cheeks, her eyes slowly closed. Pleasure sharpened the beautiful lines of her mouth and jaw, and he knew with a fierceness that surprised him that *he* had been the one to bring this strong woman to the point of surrender.

Her hands clutched at him. He wanted to lower her to the floor, remove their clothing, and take her with him on the journey to pleasure. Already her body trembled. As he circled over her center, she tightened her thighs around his hand. He lowered his mouth to hers.

But before they could kiss, the door in the next court slammed shut. With a curse of frustration, Jack knew this was neither the time nor the place for them to make love. He shifted his arm so he could continue to support Lauren and at least allow her to reach her peak, but she resisted the movement. The stiffness of her body told him she'd heard the noise next door. The outside world had violated their moment of passion. He drew his hand up before she could push him away.

Now the flush on her cheeks wasn't from pleasure, but from embarrassment.

"That shouldn't have happened," she said, turning her back on him and straightening her T-shirt. "I'm not sure why I allowed things to get out of control, but please accept my apology and my assurance that I won't—"

"Stop it." He picked up his racquet, not sure what to say. "Neither of us planned it."

She kept her back to him. "In my position, I can't afford these kinds of lapses."

"You sound as if this has happened on every job."

She glanced at him over her shoulder. "Of course not."

"Then don't regret what happened."

Her eyebrows drew together. "Why?"

"Because I don't. It's inevitable." He laughed harshly. "Now I sound like you. But you know what I mean. You feel it, too. The connection. Whatever you want to call it."

She turned slowly. Her gaze drifted down his body, pausing at the still visible proof of his words. One hand fluttered as if she would touch him, then she shook her head.

"No. You are a monogamous creature. I will not come between you and what you love."

She was right, of course. He should give up and walk away. He was playing with a fire that threatened to burn them both. But he couldn't ignore the heat. Good sense be damned.

He stepped closer to her. She flinched, but didn't back up. He raised one hand and touched her face. "I want you to warm my bed."

"And when it's over, you'll walk away without looking back?"

He dropped his hand. "Is that a problem?"

"No."

Green eyes held his own. Not by a breath or a blink did she give herself away, yet he wondered if she lied.

He pushed away the troubling thought. Lauren knew him better than any woman. She wouldn't put herself in a position to expect more than he was willing to give. Besides, he'd always been up front about his feelings on commitment.

She bent down and picked up her racquet. "I need to hit the showers. I have a meeting in less than an hour and a half."

"You want to do this again?" He chuckled at her outraged glare. "The game, not the, ah, other part."

"You mean racquetball?"

"Yeah. You want to play again? Say, Friday?"

She picked up her towel and rubbed it over her face. "Sure. I could use the practice. Who knows, by the time this is all over, I might be able to beat you."

"In a pig's eye. Lady, I went easy on you today."

"Boy, talk about challenging a guy's masculinity." For the first time since their moment of passion, she smiled. "I must have hit a nerve. Okay, Jack, we'll play Friday. And this time don't bother going easy. I don't need special favors from a guy like you."

He held open the door and allowed her to precede him. "Good, because you won't get any. If you had your way, I wouldn't even be going to my own negotiations."

She paused in the hallway and looked up at him. All the passion and embarrassment had faded, leaving her looking concerned and determined. "That wouldn't be such a bad idea. If you could give the team a chance to establish a relationship—"

He cut her off with a glance. "Don't even think about it. Baldwin International is *my* company. No one gets control but me."

She shrugged. "That's what I thought. Still, it didn't hurt to ask."

"It never does. Ask me anything you want."

"Okay. I want to ask you to listen to me."

He slipped the balls into his pocket and folded his arms over his chest. A couple of men he knew walked past them in the hallway. Jack nodded but didn't introduce Lauren. They didn't need to know anything about her, not if their interested stares were anything to go by.

"I'm listening," he said.

"No. Not now. I mean in general. Over the next couple of weeks. Don't play macho anymore. This deal is important, and if you want to be successful, you'll have to modify your normal approach."

She stared up at him so intently, he started to get uncomfortable. "Hey, lighten up," he said, then grinned. "You're my ace in the hole, kid. Of course I'm going to listen to you. Why else would I be paying you the big money?"

"Yeah. Sure." Lauren looked at him for several more seconds, then turned away. When she was about halfway down the hall, she glanced back. "You know, Jack, when you lie, you get a little twitch." She touched the corner of her eye. "Right here."

*   *   *

Lauren moved the small bouquet of flowers to the center of the table, then stood back and studied it. Too much, she thought, then picked up the arrangement and set it on the sideboard. For the second time in as many minutes, she checked that the water pitchers were full, that there were coffee, tea, and sodas to drink, and that the temperature of the room was a comfortable seventy-three degrees.

Opening-night jitters, she thought, placing one hand on her stomach. It would pass as soon as the meeting got under way. The Baldwin International team had assembled in a nearby room. Jack was giving them a last-minute pep talk. Lauren had listened as long as she could, but it had sounded more like the speech by a football coach than the last quiet, wise words of a business leader. Win at any cost, he'd told them. She shook her head in despair. She'd done her best, but he'd refused to listen. And now it was too late. The only hope lay in the team itself. If Jack gave them room in which to perform, they might be able to pull it off. If he insisted on being the show . . . She sighed. They didn't have a prayer.

The sound of conversation and footsteps drifted down the hall. Lauren forced herself to smile brightly as she turned to greet Jack and his team.

"Everything ready?" he asked as he entered the room and walked to her side.

"Yes. If I've forgotten anything, it's not for lack of keeping lists." She motioned to the sheaf of papers on the corner of the sideboard. "I've checked them about forty times."

"I have every confidence."

Around the two of them, the rest of the team moved into the room, but she only saw Jack. His blue-gray eyes darkened to the color of slate. The stark white shirt provided a perfect foil for his red power tie and handsome features. He'd slung a dark gray suit jacket over one shoulder, and she watched mesmerized as he slipped it on, then adjusted his collar. Muscles rippled and bunched with the movements.

She now knew the exact shape and feel of him pressing next to her. Although there hadn't been a repeat of the intimacy they had shared almost three weeks before on the racquetball court, every inch of her body remembered in exquisite detail the magic and passion they had generated. They had continued to play racquetball together several times a week, but it had been as colleagues, not lovers. She wanted it this way, she told herself firmly. He was her boss; she had a job to do. Any other scenario was a fantasy that would provide a one-way ticket to heartbreak. He wasn't interested in commitment, and she was incapable of giving her body without her heart trailing along for the ride.

He glanced around the room. "Looks ready enough to me." Then he frowned. "Are you sure this is the right meeting room? There's one on the next floor that has a terrific view of the lake."

"We've been over this. It's the wrong shape. The table has to be perpendicular to the door. In the other conference room, you walk in at one end, and the table runs the length of the room. Here the entrance is in the middle of the room."

"Right. The guest of honor needs to be seated farthest from the door. I remember." He studied the long table. "The two ends are equidistant from the door."

"Exactly."

The rest of the team huddled together, talking softly.

Sally approached her. "Almost time. Why are we all so nervous?"

"I'm not nervous," Jack said confidently. "You guys have worked hard. Everything will be fine. Trust me. By the end of the day, we'll have Tonikita Corporation eating out of our hands."

"But Lauren said negotiation would take several days."

Jack shrugged. "Why bother? We'll state all the reasons we're the right company for them, and let them decide." He grinned at Lauren. "Giving them an appropriate amount of time to consider their answers, of course."

"Of course," she murmured. Her hands tightened into fists. Dear God, it was crumbling right in front of her eyes. He hadn't listened to a thing she'd said, and they were about to fall on their butts in a very public, very final sort of way.

Sally glanced from Jack to Lauren. "But, Jack, I thought—"

Lauren touched her assistant's arm and shook her head. "Let it go."

"I'm going to get some coffee," Jack said. "Anybody want any?"

The two women shook their heads.

When he was gone, Sally leaned close and whispered, "I don't understand what he's talking about. I thought we'd agreed on the presentation."

"Apparently Jack is having second thoughts."

"But he can't."

"He can, Sally. The bottom line is that he *is* Baldwin International. He can do any damn thing he pleases."

Her assistant rubbed the bridge of her nose. "Then

what did he hire you for? Why have we been doing all this training?''

Lauren knew why she'd been hired. For several weeks she'd allowed herself to pretend otherwise, had thought she might be able to make a difference. But all the teaching, the lectures, the role-playing, had been wasted. The one man with the capacity for making it all work couldn't care less.

"I think that on some level, he knows we're right, but he's not willing to give up what's always worked for him in the past."

"Are you going to talk to him?"

Lauren glanced around the conference room. The team stood together by the door, Jack in the center of the circle. Everyone wore the dark, conservative suits she'd requested. Under the quiet conversation, she heard whispered words of Japanese as individuals practiced their greetings and opening statements. Tension and excitement rippled with each breath. They all wanted to win. Except Jack. He stood in the group, yet separate. In his mind, the meeting was a formality. He'd already won. Maybe she was overreacting. Maybe he was right about this and the negotiators from Tonikita Corporation *would* respond favorably to his nononsense approach.

"Talk to him?" she repeated. "No. It's his company, his deal. His chase. To the victor go the spoils."

The telephone on the sideboard buzzed. Jack picked up the receiver and spoke.

"They're here," he said, his eyes searching for, then finding, Lauren. "Let's go welcome them aboard."

SEVEN

Jack watched as Lauren moved confidently through the crowd of Japanese businessmen. Her low voice spoke their complex language easily. Bows were exchanged, and business cards. He was introduced to each member of the Tonikita team. They all understood English, although their speaking abilities varied from barely understandable to completely fluent. They had brought a translator to help with the idiosyncracies. His team would use Lauren.

The spokesperson, a man in his late forties, shook hands firmly. His intelligent brown eyes quickly took Jack's measure. Jack stood still, allowing the inspection. Snippets of Lauren's lessons drifted back to him. This was not normal procedure. An obvious assessment would be considered presumptuous. Was this an indication that the Japanese team was willing to be progressive in other areas?

"I am Mr. Watanabe," the spokesman said. "My first name is unpronounceable to most Westerners."

"Jack Baldwin."

"Mr. Baldwin. We have heard much about you. Your contract with the French was most impressive."

"You do your homework."

The man frowned for a moment, then smiled. "Ah, yes, homework. It is my job to do my homework."

Lauren spoke with the other men, but Jack felt her gaze returning to him again and again. He caught her eye and winked. She smiled. All was going smoothly. After exchanging a few more greetings, she turned to usher the men toward the elevator.

They reached the conference room without incident. Jack hung back while more introductions were made. Lauren moved between the groups, switching from Japanese to English and back, smiling gently, glossing over any slips in etiquette.

After a few awkward pauses, the two teams began to mingle. He saw Sally's curly head bob as she nodded in agreement with something a handsome, dark-suited man was saying. She spoke haltingly in Japanese. The man listened intently, then grinned and pulled a pen out of his suit pocket and handed it to her. Apparently Sally's Japanese lessons were paying off.

Lauren approached him. "Five minutes into the process, and so far, it's looking good."

Jack surveyed his employees. "This is all your doing. I'm impressed."

He felt her gaze and turned to meet her green eyes. Her suit, like everyone else's, was conservative. The long, slim skirt skimmed well past her knees. The boxy jacket hung to her hips, and the thick, moss green fabric didn't even hint at any curves below. Gleaming mahogany hair had been pulled back and braided. Even her makeup was more subdued than normal.

"Thank you," she said.

"I don't believe I've seen you wear that suit before."

She glanced down quickly, then back at him, and wrinkled her nose. "Ugly, huh?"

"I wouldn't go that far."

"I would. But it serves a purpose. I want the attention to be on the presentation and not the presenter. Besides, it shows respect. Why are you laughing?"

He continued to chuckle. "Because it doesn't work. You couldn't look frumpy no matter how hard you tried."

She seemed to relax a little. "You haven't seen me first thing in the morning."

"Not for lack of trying."

Her eyes widened. Her mouth opened, then closed as if she couldn't think of what she had been about to say. The electricity between them arced to life, burning his body with its powerful spark.

She swallowed. "Jack, this isn't the time or the place."

"I know."

"Then don't."

"You make me forget myself."

"This is your chance to win. How can you forget?"

He fought the urge to silence her questions with a kiss. The desire, totally inappropriate for the circumstances, shocked him. Was he losing it?

"I didn't forget," he said sharply. "Let's get this show going."

"Fine."

She walked toward one end of the table. Jack followed. As he opened his briefcase, the rest of the people in the room moved to take their seats.

Jack pulled out several thick files, and the copy of

the opening speech he and Lauren had written. The first paragraph was in Japanese. They'd worked for several hours perfecting his pronunciation.

When everyone was settled, he cleared his throat and began. "Honored gentlemen," he said in slow Japanese.

Lauren glanced at the clock and forced herself to exhale the breath she'd been holding. Three-thirty, day two of the meetings. So far, nothing horrible had happened. But the tension in the room—no, the tension between her and Jack—was as tangible as the table at which they sat.

He was angry and frustrated, and like any wounded animal, he was also dangerous and unpredictable.

She'd spent most of last night trying to figure out what had upset him. Perhaps her reminder yesterday that he was paying more attention to her than the chase had hit a little too close to home. But that didn't make sense. He was only interested in her for a short-term affair. Why would it matter that, for the moment, they were both a little obsessed?

Last night, lying alone in her suddenly too wide, too empty bed, she'd felt a flush on her face as the word had echoed over and over again.

Affair.

How sordid it sounded. How cheap. Not her style at all. Yet she knew he offered nothing else. A few days, make that nights, perhaps weeks, even a month or two. A fire that burned so hot, the laws of physics required it to burn itself out. When he knew all her secrets, had discovered what it was that made her attractive to him, he would then concoct an antidote and free himself of the relationship. She would be left alone—and shattered.

The price was too high. When he asked her to his bed—and knowing Jack, he *would* ask—she'd refuse. Better to be out in the cold than to risk dying in the flames.

Sally finished her presentation and sat down. Lauren forced herself to concentrate on the proceedings at hand. Jack sat on her left. She sensed his restlessness. So far, he had followed the prescribed plan, but she wondered for how much longer. He'd stopped taking notes sometime before lunch. Now he tapped his pen impatiently.

She was about to suggest a short break when he stood up. Something had snapped inside him. She saw it in the way he paced the area between the chair and the wall. Everyone looked at him expectantly.

Abruptly he turned to face the table, then placed his hands on the back of his chair. His tight features and his air of complete confidence and control warned her that the time for waiting was over. Danger signs flashed in front of Lauren. Dear God, she thought, there wasn't any escape.

"We've been talking here for almost two days," Jack began. "I think by now you should have an idea of what my company is about. But really, gentlemen, is all this necessary?"

The Japanese team glanced at one another, then at Jack. They didn't understand the question. Their translator spoke frantically for several seconds, then the room grew quiet.

"We are talking about a multimillion-dollar deal. The bottom line is, I'm the best match for your company. We have the production capacity, the know-how, and the people. That's really all that matters. Don't you agree?"

Their spokesman frowned slightly. After a short pause, he said, *"Hai."*

Jack nodded. "I knew you'd see it my way, Mr. Watanabe. I know you do things differently in Japan. And I respect that. But we're practically in the twenty-first century. Our economies are global. There's no room for pussyfooting around. If you want something, you have to grab it. I have some figures here that show the projected income from the joint venture. I think you'll find the numbers speak for themselves."

He spoke for over an hour. Even Lauren was impressed with his research and knowledge of the proposed venture. He answered the questions raised, although there weren't very many. Every time he pushed for agreement, the Japanese team responded with the word *"Hai."* Jack knew that meant yes.

What he didn't remember, or didn't care about, was that it also meant "I hear what is being said." It was not always a sign of agreement.

At one point, she'd tried to interrupt him. In a lull, while he was changing the slides in the projector, she'd suggested a brief break. He'd brushed off her comment and continued talking. It was like watching a rock roll down a mountain. The farther it traveled, the more it picked up speed, until there was nothing to do but get out of the way.

His team hung on his every word. This was the charismatic leader they'd sell their souls for. All training was forgotten as they applauded the subtleties of his proposal. The Japanese delegation shrank back at their end of the table, gradually putting more and more distance between themselves and the Americans.

At four forty-five, Jack turned off the slide projector and put down his notes.

"That about sums it up. Any questions?"

Mr. Watanabe rose to his feet. "You have told us everything we need to know."

Jack grinned. "I aim to please."

The older man studied him for a minute. "You do your job very well, Mr. Baldwin. I have no doubt of your future success in this arena." He bowed slightly, then turned to Lauren. "Kiyoshi Yamashita sends greetings to the godmother of his first male grandchild. May I tell him you are well?"

She stood and bowed deeply. "Yes. Tell him . . ." She glanced around the conference room. All the work had been for nothing. "Tell him I seek only to honor his family."

Mr. Watanabe nodded. "We will, what is the expression? Ah yes, we will be in touch."

With that, his team quickly gathered their belongings and filed out of the room.

Jack's employees sat stunned for about thirty seconds, then they exploded into conversation.

"Did you see that?" Sally asked. "He blew them out of the water. Totally amazing."

"Amazing," Lauren echoed weakly.

Hands hit in high-five salutes. Jack accepted the congratulations with good-natured modesty.

"Hey, we're a team," he said. "You guys lulled them with the fancy presentation and set them up so that I could nail them for the kill. Okay, guys, everybody across the street to Kelley's bar. Drinks are on me."

Jack waited, but she never showed up.

He set down the scotch he'd been nursing and sighed. He couldn't believe Lauren was a sore loser, but there wasn't any other explanation. Unless she was afraid of what he'd say to her.

Damn it, she had to know he'd never rub her nose in his success. Oh, he'd gloat a little, but he was entitled. After all she'd put him through, he deserved some gloat time.

With the free-flowing liquor, the rest of the team became loud and teasing, sending jokes back and forth at the speed of light. Jack signed for the bar tab and slipped away while they were busy concentrating on their victory.

He made his way across the street, then up the building elevator to the top floor of Baldwin International. Following an inner voice that told him where she was, he walked directly to Lauren's office.

The light shining through the open door indicated that she was still there. He stepped into the room. The lamp on the floor by the couch illuminated half the room, but the part where she stood, in front of the window, was in shadow. Open drapes allowed a view of the city at night. Lights shone out from windows, car headlights flickered some forty stories below. The lake faded into darkness beyond the high-rises.

But it was the woman who drew his attention. She'd abandoned her moss-colored suit jacket. The white, filmy blouse draped intimately over her shoulders and back, outlining the delicate structure of her body. A narrow waist flared into rounded hips. The skirt hid her legs from view, but he remembered her in shorts. Lean thighs flowed into curvy calves. He tugged at his collar as the temperature in the room seemed to climb about ten degrees.

Instead of the teasing comment he'd planned, he

found himself walking quietly up behind her and simply speaking her name.

"Lauren?"

"How was the party?" she asked without turning around.

"Lonely without you."

"I'm sure you had enough admirers willing to hang on your every word."

"I never thought you'd be a sore loser."

She laughed. The harsh sound had nothing to do with humor. "I was raised by a general and with two large, older brothers. I know all about losing with grace. This isn't about losing."

"Then what?"

"You think you've won; now you've come to claim your prize."

He didn't like the bitterness in her voice. "It's never been like that."

"Oh. Are you sure? What have I been to you if not a challenge?"

"I don't deserve that," he said, fighting the guilt that surged through him. "You've been an integral part of the team. We couldn't have done this without you."

"No, Jack. That's where you're wrong. You could have done just as well, or should I say just as badly, on your own. You needed me to give you an in with Yamashita, nothing more. I should have saved us both a lot of trouble and simply sold you the rights to my name."

"Wait a minute. That's not fair. You worked damn hard on this project."

"For nothing."

She turned to look at him. In the faint light from

the floor lamp he could see two faint tracks down her cheeks.

"You're crying." Confusion filled him. And concern. "What's wrong?"

"I'm *not* crying." She jerked her head away when he tried to touch her, and brushed her face with the back of her hand. "Damn it, I refuse to cry over this. Or you."

"What are you talking about?"

"You don't get it."

"Get what?"

She folded her arms over her chest. "You didn't win in there, Jack. The Tonikita team isn't going to call tomorrow and offer you a deal. The only thing you're going to get from them is a polite letter explaining that your business styles don't match and that it will be best for everyone to just put this incident behind you. Oh, and they'll wish you luck with future ventures."

He smiled gently and took a step closer. Her perfume surrounded him with a soft floral fragrance. "Lauren, you're wrong. Watanabe and his group were very impressed with all of us. You heard him. He said he has no doubt of our future success."

"Not 'our'. Your. I tried to warn you what would happen if you insisted on doing this your way."

Why was she refusing to see the truth? he wondered. There wasn't a doubt in his mind he'd done the right thing. For almost two days he'd sat through presentations and proper etiquette. But in the end, the numbers spoke for themselves. Tonikita Corporation couldn't afford to walk away from what he was offering. There wasn't another company in the country—hell, the world—who could touch him.

"It's a done deal," he said.

"It's over. For both of us."

"What does that mean?"

"We've both failed." She reached up and touched his cheek. "But I accept the responsibility. I should have been able to find a way to make you believe me. You never took me or what I had to say seriously."

Her fingers moved gently against his skin, rasping against the stubble, sliding sensuously toward his mouth. He turned his head toward her palm and silently encouraged the caress, but she dropped her hand.

"The bottom line," she said, not meeting his eyes, "is that you've never taken me seriously."

"I have." But the lie sat heavily on his lips.

"No, you haven't. I understand that. I will say in your defense that it's not because I'm a woman. You're fair in that."

He drew his brows together. "Lauren, you've completely lost me. I'm sorry I didn't play the game your way through till the end, but you did teach me a lot. And the team. Like I said, we couldn't have done it without you."

She looked back out the window. Her arms folded over her chest. "Thanks for the words of praise. I hope you'll still mean them tomorrow."

"What could change my mind?"

"Everything."

"Don't go all mystic on me, kid. We've got some celebrating to do."

"I can't."

"Sorry, but this is one time I'm not taking no for an answer."

"That sounds familiar. Yet another example of you not listening." She glanced down, but he saw the slight smile at the corner of her mouth.

"I listen all the time."

"Right. And then you do exactly what you want."

"Only sometimes. Come on, let me take you to dinner."

"What is it?" she asked him, shaking her head. "What do you hear?"

He frowned. "What are you talking about?"

She looked up at him. "Inside your head. What makes you do this? Is it control? Trust? Who hurt you so badly that every situation can only be your way?"

He took a step back. "I don't know who you've been talking to—"

"No one," she said, turning away. "Never mind. It was stupid of me to think there was some reason." She shrugged. "It's your game. You make the rules."

He didn't like her probing at him like that. She was hitting much too close to home. But he also hated the quiver in her voice. "You're my best trade," he said, hoping the joke would make her feel better.

She raised her face. Those wide eyes, devoid of any color in the half-light, met his own. In the brief heartbeat before she blinked, he saw into her soul. The raw pain there stunned him into silence. Who had hurt her? Him? Someone on the team? Then he realized she wasn't being a sore loser at all. For some reason known only to God and maybe a few Zen believers, she really thought he'd messed up the deal. She was hurting because she thought she'd failed him. He shouldn't be pleased that she was in pain, but her concern eased his tension.

"I thought you were kidding," he said.

"About?"

"Blowing the deal. You really mean it."

"Yes. Yes." Relief filled her voice. "Don't you see?

They were just being polite. *Hai* means more than just agreement, it also means—"

He cut her off. "Trust me, Lauren. I've been doing this for years. I can smell a crashed deal at fifty miles. We're in."

She closed her eyes and sighed. "There's nothing I can say to convince you, is there?"

"Nope." He grinned. "Now, how about that dinner?"

She shook her head. "I'm tired."

"I won't keep you out late."

"I'm not dressed for anywhere decent."

"No problem. We'll swing by your place and you can put on something pretty." He leaned forward and brushed her mouth with his. As he'd hoped, the fire was still smoldering under the surface. It flamed into life and singed the first layer of his skin. "Or better yet, sexy."

"There's nothing to celebrate," she said, but her resolve was weakening. He could tell by the way her tongue came out and traced her lower lip, as if to hold on to the brief contact.

"I don't need an excuse. What if we agree not to talk about what happened today? Come on, Godzilla-eyes. We've both earned it."

She studied him thoroughly. Her gaze catalogued each of his features. When he was sure she was about to give in, she placed her hands on his chest and raised herself up on her toes and kissed him.

"No."

She picked up her jacket and briefcase, then walked away without a word.

This situation was what her mother would have called "paying the piper." The general would have told her running away never won a war. But it cuts down on casualties, Lauren thought. Still, leaving like that had been a gesture at best. Her head start was less than five minutes. By the time she reached her quiet neighborhood, Jack was on her tail. She watched him drive up behind her. Her rearview mirror reflected his anger and the impatient tapping of his fingers on the steering wheel. She thought about driving past her house, circling into one of the local shopping centers, and trying to lose him in the parking lot. No, she thought. Running was one thing, hiding quite another.

She pulled into her driveway and hit the button on the automatic garage door opener. After parking her car, she closed the garage door, then entered the house and walked straight to the front. He was already waiting on the porch.

She released the lock and walked into the kitchen. The front door flew open.

"What the hell was that all about?" he demanded as he entered her house. "Of all the cowardly, uptight—" He stood in the kitchen door and glared. "I never pegged you as the type to walk away from a fight."

That one hurt, she thought as she tried not to flinch. She reached in the refrigerator and pulled out a soda. Without offering him one, she popped open the can and drank.

He continued to stand there, staring at her. She couldn't ignore him forever. If she thought for a moment he'd go away . . . But he wouldn't. Not when she'd wounded his male pride.

She leaned against the sink and studied the linoleum floor. It needed washing, she thought. And there was ironing. The mundane tasks of life never went away, no matter how badly her personal life went.

"I shouldn't have walked out like that," she said at last.

The sound of his breathing was the only response.

"There didn't seem to be another alternative," she added. "I felt trapped."

"By me?"

"By the situation."

"In what way?"

He'd relaxed a little. She could hear it in his voice. "I can't explain."

"Then come to dinner."

"Why?"

He paused. "Because I need you. And you need me, too."

There it was again. That word. He'd said it before. She'd assumed he'd been kidding. Apparently she'd been wrong. *Want* would have been easy to resist. *Want*, she understood. Men often wanted women. It was a biological urge, like wanting a glass of water on a hot day. But *need*. Ah, that was something else again. Did she need him? Was he necessary for her survival or her well-being? Could she go on as well as—no, better than—before if she walked away from him?

She continued to study the floor, counting the number of squares that made up the width of her kitchen. Jack shifted in the doorway. She hoped that he'd say something to explain his statement, that he would erase the power of the word "need" with something charming and inane. No such luck.

"I think this is the first time I've seen you speechless," he said quietly.

"I can't play this game with you."

"I'm not playing."

Slowly she raised her eyes. He stood tall in the doorway, his arms folded over his chest. Every inch of him screamed male. His mouth pulled into a straight line. He wasn't teasing her. This time he was telling the truth: He wasn't playing.

"It's never been a game, Lauren," he said. "However much we both want to pretend it is." His blue-gray eyes met and held hers. "I just want to have dinner with you. Is that so awful?"

She bit her lower lip. "There's liquor in that cupboard," she said, pointing. "Fix yourself a drink." With that, she walked quickly past him and down the hall.

"Was that a 'yes'?" he called after her.

"Yes."

She was a fool, she told herself firmly as she entered her bedroom and shut the door. Worse, she was willingly walking into a situation that was going to break her heart and threaten her career. People had been institutionalized for less.

So why was she agreeing to this dinner with Jack? She could still say no. Her father liked to remind her it had been the first word she'd ever learned. She was good at saying no. She rejected men's invitations all the time.

From the living room came the sound of ice tinkling in a glass as Jack prowled the room.

"Why him?" she asked her reflection in the mirrored closet door. "Why did it have to be him?"

There wasn't an answer. Which was probably good, she thought, daring to smile. Bad enough to be stupid, worse to hear voices.

It would come tomorrow or the next day. Thinly

bracketed by polite words and careful phrases, they would reject him and his Western ways. He would feel she betrayed him twice. First by not making him successful and second by not convincing him that the deal was lost. She had played her cards as best she could, but the dealer had twenty-one, and there wasn't a damn thing she could do about it.

Dear God, she was starting to think like him. She leaned her forehead against the cool closet door and sighed. Her breath fogged a small circle. She traced a letter, then a heart around the tiny *J*. He was lost to her already. So why not take what was offered?

Perhaps he really did mean to take her to dinner and nothing more. Yet in his mind, the deal had been won. There wasn't any reason for a restriction on their relationship. He would want to claim her. If not tonight, then soon. Did she dare allow him, allow *herself*, to give in? She knew the truth. She knew what was to come. Would he hate her more—or less—if she made love with him?

"I want him," she whispered to her reflection.

A statement closer to the truth might be that she loved him, but she wasn't ready to admit that yet, she thought. Not even to herself. Tonight—it was their only chance to be together. Her one opportunity to play with the fantasy of what might have been, had Jack been another sort of man, or she a different woman.

She had joined his team because she was tired of always taking the safe road. It had been time to make a change. Risk didn't always mean something bad. Hadn't she learned anything from that lesson?

Lauren stepped back and unzipped her skirt. While it fell to the floor, she started on the buttons of her blouse. She slid open the closet and stared at the contents. *Sexy*, he'd said. How sexy? An "I know we're going to do it tonight, so I'm dressing to make it easy" sort of outfit, or maybe a more subtle "look at all these buttons and won't you have fun undoing them" kind of look.

She pulled out a dark peach strapless number, then shook her head and put it back. There were her black gabardine pants and an off-the-shoulder sweater. Maybe a—

"Oh, hell, nothing is this important." She pulled off her panty hose and grabbed her robe. After slipping it on and tying the sash in a bow, she started down the hall.

"Jack," she called before she got to the living room. "Where are we going for dinner? I don't know what to wear."

She crossed the threshold into the room and paused. He glanced at her.

He stood beside her sculpture, as if he'd been studying the lines of the artwork. His tie was gone and he'd undone the first three buttons of his shirt. Curly dark hairs peeked out from the open vee. As was his usual mode for the end of the workday, his sleeves had been rolled up to his elbows. Black hair, ruffled by fingers being run through the thick length, tumbled over his forehead. Blue-gray eyes deepened to the color of smoke. Slowly he raised the glass to his lips and took a sip. She watched as the muscles in his throat contracted, then released as he swallowed.

Then he looked at her. Really looked. From the top of her head, where her hair was still pulled back in a french braid, down her calf-length robe, to her bare feet, where her toes curled into the carpet.

The heat of his attention burned to her core.

"I like what you're wearing now," he said. "We don't have to go anywhere at all."

A blush stole across her cheeks. She felt as awkward as a virgin on her wedding night. "But aren't you hungry?" she blurted out, then could have moaned with mortification when he smiled.

"Yes."

"I meant—"

"I know what you meant, Lauren."

The man had disappeared, and in his place stood the predator. The lines of his face sharpened, deepening the hollows of his cheeks. She stood almost ten feet away, but was aware of the steady rise and fall of his chest, as if his breathing had become more labored. He set his drink on the coffee table.

"Undo the braid," he said, as he took a single step towards her.

"Jack, I—"

He took another step. "Take your hair down. Please. Or tell me no."

No. There was that word again. The one she was supposed to be so good at. For more than a month she'd played the waiting game with Jack, had teased and been teased, aroused him and been aroused. She knew she matched him intellect for intellect, wit for wit. Yet all that ceased to matter. He was her mate, she was his to claim. Or refuse.

No. One syllable—so easy to say. Too easy. She reached up and behind her neck for the ribbon tied around the tail of her braid.

He took another step closer. Her fingers shook as she pulled the ribbon loose and let it fall to the floor. His eyes held her captive. She no longer had the capacity to decide. As she loosened the strands, he took another step. Less than two feet separated them. She held her breath and waited for his touch.

He smiled, exposing the dimple on his right cheek. "It's not going to be that easy, Lauren. I've waited for you longer, and wanted you more, than any other woman in my life."

She simply stared. What was she supposed to say to that? Her first thought was that it was all a line designed to get her into his bed. She dismissed the idea. Jack would never need to use a line—on her or any other woman.

"Only you, Lauren," he said, as if he could read her mind. "Trust me."

"I do."

"Then finish taking down your hair. I like it best down. I like the way the light catches the different colors. I've never known a woman with your color hair." He spoke softly, slowly, as if they were the last two people alive and had all the time they would ever need. Each word brushed against her skin, sensitizing nerve endings. Her heart beat faster, her body felt hot.

She freed the last of the braid and finger-combed her hair.

"Bring it forward, over your shoulders," he said.

She did as he requested, and smoothed the strands over her shoulders and down her chest. The ends reached to her breasts. One curl tickled her neck. She arched her head and exhaled.

"You are beautiful," he said. "Untie your robe."

She hesitated.

"Come to me," he said. "Or not. It's always been up to you. Didn't you know?" Despite his almost sad half smile, his gaze smoldered against her. The look was as tangible as a touch. He probed the shadowed valley between her breasts. "Untie your robe. Show yourself to me, or tell me you don't want to make love."

She'd never been with a man like him before. The rules were unfamiliar. He demanded that she be an equal. There could be no morning-after recriminations or excuses that she'd been swept away by the moment. She was to be with him by choice, or not at all.

"I'm afraid." She spoke softly.

"Of me?"

Easy question. Jack might frustrate her and make her want to wring his neck at times, but fear him? She shook her head. "No."

"Of yourself?"

That question was harder. Did she fear herself? Did she know she teetered on the edge of a precipice? Did she sense all previous roads in her life led to this moment? To this man?

She shrugged her response.

"Of what might happen?" he asked.

She looked away. "Yes."

"Do you trust me?"

"With my life," she said, echoing his response from a few days ago. And with her heart, she thought to herself.

"I'd like to see your body," he said simply.

She reached for the sash of her robe. It came loose easily, and the silken garment fell open. His intake of breath was audible in the still room. He reached out one hand as if he might touch that which he could now see. His fingers stirred the air in front of her breasts, inducing a whispered current that cooled her heated flesh. She could feel her nipples pressing against the lacy cup of her bra. Her midsection grew heavy with desire, and moisture dampened her panties.

She tossed her head, at once proud, yet shy to bare herself in front of him. Never had a man made so many demands on her. In the past, sex, especially the first time with someone, had been quick and fumbling. Not that she had so many experiences with which to compare. But with Jack. She licked her lower lip. His eyes dilated. There was nothing fumbling about it or him.

"Tell me you want me," he said, his voice gravelly with need.

She answered him without words. After easing the robe off her shoulders, she straightened her arms and allowed the garment to fall to the floor. The silk brushed against her back and thighs as it dropped. It was as if Jack himself had touched her.

He groaned at the sight of her near-nakedness. Only the lace of her bra and panties covered her. With one stride, he crossed the area between them, stopping inches away.

"I never imagined anyone like you," he said.

"Then you don't have much of an imagination." She smiled.

He didn't. "Don't. Don't mock yourself or your beauty. You are precious to me." He reached up and traced her lips with his index finger. Her body ached to feel his, her skin longed to press nakedness against nakedness. Her mind yearned to hear more and more of his words, for he was seducing her without touch.

"I want you," he said.

She opened her mouth and moistened the tip of his finger with her tongue. Their eyes met. Fire smoldered. He tasted salty, yet sweet. With their gazes locked, she drew his finger inside and circled him with her tongue.

It was their only point of contact. When he would have withdrawn. she bit down to keep him in place.

"There's a price for playing with me."

"I'll risk it," she said, releasing him.

He drew the damp finger over her chin and down her throat, making a straight line toward the valley between her breasts. Before she could catch her breath, he flicked open the center hook of her bra. The cups parted, but clung on to her puckered nipples.

He bent over and kissed her between her breasts. Her knees threatened to buckle.

"You are mine," he said, then bent and lifted her into his arms.

EIGHT

He carried her into her bedroom, then lowered her onto the bed. Before her head hit the pillow, his mouth claimed hers. Hunger drove him to consume her, and she responded in kind.

Lips parted instantly. Tongues plunged and circled and dueled. His taste and scent surrounded her. Arms reached and brushed and clung. Both of his hands held her head, his fingers threaded through her hair and pressed into her scalp. She tugged at his shirt, struggling to pull it off while it was still buttoned. One of his legs settled between hers, and she felt the pressure of his erection against her hip.

In that instant, she knew she would cease to exist if he did not fill her. Their joining was as vital to her as her next breath.

He withdrew his tongue, then circled her lips, dipping in to sample the tender flesh. When she moaned, he swallowed the sound.

Her breasts strained against the partial coverage of

her bra. She shifted and used the friction of his shirt to bare her chest, then she moved from side to side, sliding the hardened tips against him. This time he moaned.

His hands moved down her cheeks. One after the other, he touched his fingers to her mouth. She licked and sucked and bit each in turn. His smoldering gaze promised her a journey beyond measure to a place she had never imagined. For a split second she wondered about finding her way back. Would he abandon her in the foreign land? Then he rose up on his knees, straddled her hips, and moved his hands to her breasts. All conscious thought ended.

There was only the moment and the man and the endless pleasurable sensation he created with his fingers and tongue. Every inch of her breasts received his full attention. He nibbled and laved as though he'd been deprived three lifetimes. When he sucked on her nipples, she bit her lip to hold back the scream of pleasure.

"Don't," he whispered. "I want to hear you."

She shook her head in refusal. He moved to the other breast and flicked his tongue against the taut peak. Her hands clutched the bedspread. Her knees rose.

"Do it," he murmured against her skin. "Be as wild as you want. Say anything you want. You can't shock me, Lauren. I know who you are."

His fingers danced on her hardened peaks. She arched toward his touch.

"You like this," he said.

She nodded once, focusing only on the sensations.

"Tell me," he demanded, then drew her hard nipple into his mouth.

"What?" she gasped.

"Tell me you like it."

He closed his teeth until she felt the slight pressure on her taut flesh. She inhaled, not in fear or pain but from the torture of being on the edge. "I . . ."

He bit a little more. His hand cupped her other breast and held the full curve in his palm. Forefinger and thumb mimicked the action of his mouth.

"I like it," she ground out, and tightened the muscles in her hips and thighs. How much more could she stand? How could she ever have resisted this pleasure?

He moved lower; wet kisses trailed to her navel. He dipped inside. She forced her lips together, not daring to give in to the sound building up within her. Part of her wondered at his need for her to verbalize her pleasure; part of her longed to give in to his request. In the past, she'd always been quiet. But there was something about his primal touch. It was the appeal of a virile man determined to pleasure his woman.

When he reached the barrier of her panties, he gripped the elastic and peeled them down. His large hands made the return journey slowly, rubbing along her calves and thighs. He massaged deeply, sweeping his thumbs up the inside of her legs until the tips brushed the mahogany curls.

He teased her, moving closer and closer, but never touching her most sensitive spot. She held her breath and flexed her hips to encourage him, but still he tormented her. At last he lay back down beside her. While he nuzzled her breasts, his right hand stroked her lower stomach.

Touch me there! she screamed silently.

His hand stopped moving, and for a horrified second, she thought she'd said the words aloud. No, it was only his infuriating habit of reading her mind.

"Would you like me to . . ." He trailed his fingers toward her swollen center.

"Yes!" She parted her legs.

Still he didn't touch her. She looked at him.

"I need to know that you want this," he said. "I need you to see that you make me tremble." He shrugged, his face unreadable. "I need this to be for the both of us."

Tears burned under her lids, but she blinked them away. "I want you, Jack. I want us to be together."

"Thank you," he whispered, then touched her.

She screamed. Not long or especially loud, but enough to shock herself. Still, she couldn't hold back. The pleasure shot through her with all the intensity of lightning. It raced up her midsection, down her legs, and burned the bottom of her feet.

He moved confidently, circling her tingling core, dipping into her wetness, like a bee seeking the sweetest flower. His fingers brushed the protective folds and slipped down to trace where her legs met her torso. His mouth sought hers; his tongue matched the movement of his hand and began to move to slow circles.

He touched the tiny center of her pleasure. A shiver racked her body. Gently at first, exquisitely careful never to press too hard or too long, he began to pleasure her. His fingers danced on her. He forced her to climb higher and closer until she knew she would tumble into ecstasy, then he slowed and let her float back down. He led her to the edge, then blocked the fall. When she gasped her need, he dropped his head to tend to her breasts, circling around and around until she could do nothing but focus on the magic he produced. Through it all, he showed her a depth of sensation, a stretching of her personal boundaries of need and desire, that she had never known.

Perspiration covered her body. Her nipples throbbed in time with each touch of his tongue. Heat built until the flames consumed her. At last she approached the edge with such startling speed that she feared for her life if he didn't let her fall. The need to complete what had been started dominated every fiber of her being. He moved faster and faster. She rotated her hips in time with him. And at the last, when she was terrified he would hold her back again, she clutched at him.

"Jack," she whispered. "Now."

He led her to the edge and pushed. She hung suspended for a brief moment that felt like an eternity. The pleasure was so intense that relief felt fatal—and inevitable. She had come before, but not like this. Not with an explosion that ripped her apart. Not with a scream that filled the room and made her willing to sell her soul, or her heart.

He caught the pieces, reassembled them, and held her until the shaking stopped. She kept her eyes closed, afraid of his smile or humor, shocked that she had exposed herself so fully.

Strong fingers traced her face and neck, touched her breasts and thighs. Warm breath fanned her.

"You're more beautiful than I imagined," he said.

She risked opening her eyes. He wasn't smiling, or looking remotely amused. He looked . . . content.

"Are you all right?" he asked.

She nodded.

Slate gray eyes held hers. "It's never been like that for me," he said. "You make me feel like I could conquer the world."

"It's never been like that for me, either." She

touched his mouth. "Magic. Bottle it and you could make a fortune."

"I have enough money. What I don't have enough of is you."

He bent toward her mouth. She kissed him back, and clutched at his shoulders, then pushed him away.

"You're not even undressed!"

He grinned. "I had other things on my mind."

"It's not fair that only I'm naked."

"Why?" He rose up on one elbow and stared at her breasts. "I like it."

"Maybe I want to do a little looking of my own."

"Do you?"

The shyness returned, but she ignored it. "Yes."

"That's all you had to say."

He rose and tugged his shirt free of his pants. Before she could offer to help, he'd opened the buttons and was sliding his arms free. Shoes, socks, trousers, and briefs quickly followed. He sat down on the bed, then bent over and retrieved a foil packet from his pants pocket.

"So you planned on getting lucky," she said, not sure if she was insulted or flattered. "Or are you always prepared?"

"I *was* a Boy Scout," he teased as he shifted until he faced her. Then he grew serious. "I'd hoped we'd do this. And I think too much of you to take risks with your body."

"Thank you." She sat up and kissed him. If there had been any lingering doubts, he'd effectively silenced them with his concern.

"You're welcome. And to clear the air, I don't like the phrase 'get lucky.' You make me sound like some sailor cruising bars after six months at sea."

"Sorry." She ran her fingers down his chest and back up again. The crinkly hair tickled her fingers. "I didn't mean to offend your delicate sensibilities."

"You're making fun of me."

"I think you're doing that all on your own."

Her release had given her more than pleasure; it had provided her with a freedom she'd never experienced before. There was nothing she couldn't say to Jack, nothing she couldn't confess or mock. They'd passed the place of secrets.

Her hand moved lower, over his flat stomach, down the narrowing strip of hair to the place where the band widened and his erect need pressed against her thigh.

"I'll have you know," he said, between kisses along her jaw, "that I don't appreciate this conversation."

She took him in her hand. He stiffened, then groaned. She moved back and forth in long, slow strokes. After moistening her thumb, she brushed it gently against the tip.

With her free hand, she took the foil package from him. "We don't have to be having a conversation at all."

"Fine," he said. With one swipe of his arm, he lowered her to her back. Before she could catch her breath, the protection had been used and he was nudging at her thighs. She shifted to welcome him.

Bracing his weight on his arms, he pressed home. His length stretched and pushed against her slick walls. It had been a long time.

He swore, the vulgar curse word exciting her with its intensity as well as the surprise of hearing it.

"Am I hurting you?" he asked as he flexed his hips to fill her completely.

"No." She shifted to accommodate him. "I like it."

"Good. 'Cause you're damn near killing me." His eyes narrowed to slits. "I was going to impress you with my performance, lady, but your body is about to reduce me to a first-time teenager." He withdrew and gritted his teeth.

"I'm already impressed."

One corner of his mouth quirked up. 'Yeah?"

"Yeah." She grabbed his buttocks and urged him closer, wanting him deep inside again. "Show me what you've got, sailor."

He did. The thrusts grew faster and faster. He rested his weight on his legs and leaned forward to tease her breasts. Her legs wrapped around his hips as if to keep him from escaping. Pleasure hardened his features into a mask, but soon the fires within her own body forced her to close her eyes and concentrate on the feel of him gliding in and out of her, and the rapid fluttering of his fingers on her nipples.

The climax caught her off guard. One minute she was moaning her pleasure, the next she couldn't catch her breath. As Jack thrust deeper and harder, her muscles convulsed around him. She opened her eyes, and their gazes locked. The release of her body forced him over the edge. She watched him fall, taking pleasure in the sounds he made as he stiffened within her.

A tear rolled down her temple, then another. She didn't feel like crying, but she was. He raised one hand and touched the dampness.

"Me, too, Lauren," he said, and leaned forward to kiss her. "Me, too."

"And then," Jack prompted.

"And then I graduated from high school. Why are

you insisting on a day-by-day account of my life in Japan? It was boring even for me, and I lived it.''

Lauren picked up her pint carton of ice cream and dipped in her spoon. They sat in her bed, eating junk food and reveling in the afterglow of their lovemaking. Jack leaned against the headboard; she sat facing him, her hips level with his knees. He hadn't allowed her to dress, or even pull off the bedspread so that she could hide under a sheet. Actually being naked wasn't all that bad, except for her natural inclination to sit cross-legged. When she instinctively assumed that position, Jack had smacked his lips so suggestively, she'd clamped her knees together.

"You must have been smart," he said.

"Why do you say that?"

"You got into Tokyo University. I've heard it's tough for natives, let alone Americans."

She shrugged. "I wasn't the top in my class, but I did well enough."

"Not top? So you were second?"

"No."

"Tell me."

"No."

He leaned forward and held his spoon over her right breast. Chocolate ice cream collected on the end and prepared to drip.

"Stop it," she demanded.

"Then tell me."

"All right, I was fourth."

He pulled back the spoon and licked it clean. "Out of?"

"A few hundred."

"Huh, beauty and brains, but I already knew that."

She frowned. "You're being awfully nice to me. Are you always this friendly after the, ah, act?"

He leaned forward and gave her a quick kiss that tasted of chocolate. "Lady, that was not an act."

"Jack!"

"Tell me more about Japan. Was college better than high school?"

"You mean did I fit in better?"

He nodded.

"Sort of. I was better at the language. All things American were pretty popular with the students, and I got to bask in that. It's not as if I could hide in a crowd."

He reached forward and touched her hair. "Red-headed Godzilla-eyes. You must have hated it."

"I just felt different. I don't think being a blonde would have helped much."

"You fit in now."

"Sometimes."

That was a lie. She fit perfectly, in Jack's arms if not his life. Their easy banter and physical closeness made her want to hope, but she was afraid. Afraid that he would leave her, afraid that she would be hurt, and most afraid that she would start to believe in something that could never exist.

"So tell me about the boyfriends."

"Why? You tell me about the women in *your* life."

He shrugged. "They're all boring next to you. Besides, you've studied my past exploits and already made up your mind."

"I'm sure they weren't *all* recorded in the press."

"No, but they're all about the same."

"There wasn't anyone special?"

He shrugged, then frowned. "Not that I remember. You know me."

"Yes," she said, then thought that she didn't. It was hard to believe that no woman had been able to reach inside and touch his heart. And if his reputation was anything to go by, it wasn't for women's lack of trying.

"What about you?" he asked.

"Me?"

"Yeah. Any old boyfriends about to come pounding on the door?"

"Not really. I had the usual crushes. A couple of semiserious boyfriends, nothing out of the ordinary."

"And you never got married."

"Never got asked."

His eyes sought hers. "Would you have said yes, if one of them had asked?"

She thought about Jiro. She had assumed they would marry and live together in Japan, perhaps moving to the States for a few years to further their careers. She recalled the hours they'd spent talking about what America was really like and the cultural differences between them. Looking back, with the wisdom of time on her side, she saw that he had spent most of their relationship pumping her for information. From the beginning, he'd used her.

"I might have," she admitted at last. "But it would have been a mistake."

"I'm glad you didn't."

"Are you?" She was surprised. "Why would it matter?"

He drew back in mock indignation. "I never get involved with married women."

"All these rules. How do you keep them straight?"

"I have a large staff of well-paid employees."

She jabbed him with her foot.

"What was that for?" he asked.

"To keep you in line. You're much too self-satisfied to stand."

"I was good, wasn't I?" He raised his eyebrows. "Come on, you want to tell me."

"You're a show-off, and I'm not going to contribute to your already swelled head."

"But it wasn't my head that—"

She jabbed him again. "Don't say it."

"As long as we both know what swelled."

"We do." She glanced at him. "What about you? I know what I've read in the papers, but there must be more to your past than the thumbnail sketch they give."

He shrugged. "Not really. After my mom died—"

"How old were you?" she interrupted.

"Twelve."

"I didn't know you were that young."

"It's been a long time."

"Maybe." She studied her dessert. "It must have affected you."

"I suppose. My father was gone just as much after her death as before, so I was sent away. Prep school, then college. Happens to a lot of kids. It's no big deal." He swallowed a mouthful of the ice cream. "You know the rest."

She wanted to pursue this line of questioning. There was something haunting in the way he refused to admit the loneliness of a twelve-year-old boy. She suspected there was a connection between that lonely child and the man who wouldn't let anyone inside emotionally. She wanted to ask why, but their intimacy was too new. There was only this night and perhaps another until . . .

Refusing to let herself dwell on unpleasantness, she took another spoonful of her pralines-and-cream ice cream, then scooted around until she was sitting next to him, with her back against the headboard. Their bare bodies pressed together from shoulder to thigh. She marveled at his complete lack of embarrassment, sitting there naked. She still didn't have the nerve to glance down at herself, knowing that her whole body was on display, but it wasn't difficult at all to look at him.

His long legs stretched several inches past hers. She'd seen them before, when they'd played racquetball, but had never felt the freedom to stare to her heart's content. Touch, even, if she wanted to.

Testing her theory, she rested her hand on top of his thigh. He glanced over and smiled, then offered her a taste of his ice cream. She licked the spoon.

They continued to eat in companionable silence. She glanced at his lap, shyly studying the proof of his gender. Unaroused, his male organ lay seemingly harmless in its nest of dark curls. Before when she'd touched it, she'd felt silk wrapped around engorged steel. The evidence of his need had excited her. Now, his relaxed state made her feel tender, yet confident that she could bring him to hardness with a word, or a look, or a touch.

After setting her ice cream carton on her nightstand beside the bed, she took a drink of water and rolled onto her knees.

"What are you doing?" Jack asked as she nudged his knees apart and knelt between his legs.

"Nothing."

"Lauren, you are *not* doing nothing."

She ran her hands up and down his powerful thighs,

then gently touched his penis. "Just go on with what you're doing."

"What about what you're doing?"

"I just wanted a little dessert with my dessert."

She bent over and took him in her mouth.

He stiffened, then arched his hips toward her. "Is this your way of saying you want more?"

She raised her head. "No. This is my way of saying I want you."

"I'm yours for the taking."

She smiled. "I know."

It was after midnight when they surfaced again. This time they'd pulled back the bedspread, and now the sheets tangled at the foot of the bed. Jack held her close.

"You're going to be the death of me."

"Quit complaining. You work out enough. Sex shouldn't be a problem."

"I'm not complaining." He brushed her hair away from her face and kissed her forehead. "And this wasn't sex."

She snuggled closer, enjoying the sound of his heart beating steadily beneath her ear and the fuzzy tickling of his chest hair rubbing against her cheek. "Gee, it's exactly what my mother explained sex was when we had our little talk years ago. Are you saying she was lying?"

"I find it hard to believe your mother described this particular sequence of events to anyone, let alone her daughter."

"Well, maybe not exactly *this*, but something really close."

"You're an incredible woman," he said, pulling her tight against him in a hug. "I'm lucky I found you."

She held her breath. In an evening of shared bodies and souls, they'd come to a place of sharing hearts. Would he speak of affection and commitment? Did she dare confess that she'd been thinking of staying around longer than the job required? Was it possible that they would be able to find a bit of permanence in a world dependent on obsolescence?

"Me, too," she whispered, trying to encourage him, but not willing to take the first step.

But instead of saying anything else, he released her and sat up on the edge of the bed.

"Where are you going?" she asked.

"Nature calls."

He reached down and pulled the sheets over her body. She closed her eyes and concentrated on the pleasurable tingles still rippling through her body. He was a terrific lover, she thought, then giggled at her understatement. She didn't know all the words to describe him. Tender, patient, focused . . . She sighed. She could go on for hours. Maybe in the morning, they'd make love again. At racquetball, he was always teasing her about male energy peaking around dawn. She wouldn't mind if he peaked a little with her in the A.M.

The bathroom door opened. She raised one eyelid, then scrambled into a sitting position.

"You're dressed!" She didn't even try to keep the shock out of her voice.

"Yeah." He glanced down at his shirt and trousers. "I wouldn't want to get arrested for driving home naked."

"I don't understand." She pulled the sheet up until it covered her to her shoulders. "You're leaving?"

"Lauren, it's late." He sat on the edge of the bed and picked up his socks. "We've both put in a long couple of days."

"You're not going to sleep here?"

"I don't spend the night." He smiled gently. "Please understand."

"Understand? That it's okay to make love, but you don't commit yourself to even a single night? Sure I understand. No problem." She knew her voice was rising in pitch and volume, but she couldn't control herself. How dare he? At least Jiro had been decent enough to spend the night.

"It's not personal," he insisted, his dark eyes apologizing.

"It's damn personal," she said. "Or didn't any of this matter to you?"

He reached out to touch her face, but she jerked away. He settled for stroking her arm. "It mattered. You matter. Please believe that."

She drew in a deep breath. Life in the fast lane had never been her style. Now she remembered why. High speeds frightened her. The possibilities for a crash and burn were always higher when you went too fast. She shouldn't be surprised; Jack was acting in character. She was the one out of line.

She rose from the bed and picked up her robe. After slipping it on, she tied the sash, then forced herself to smile at him. "I'm sorry. You're right. Of course you can leave. I was surprised, but it makes perfect sense."

"Are you sure? I can stay if it's that important to you."

He mouthed the correct words, but his body language—he was stepping into his shoes as he spoke—told her what he really wanted.

"It's not important at all," she lied.

She led him down the long hallways and to the front door. He grabbed his suit jacket and slung it over one shoulder.

"We had us a helluva night," he said as he cupped her chin.

"Agreed."

"Go ahead and take tomorrow off. I gave the rest of the team the day off as well. You deserve it most."

She wanted to scream at him. Despite his focused sensitivity in bed, out of it he was the same old Jack. Even after what they'd shared, business came first. Why had she allowed herself to think otherwise? It would hurt too much to say anything to him, and she refused to let him see how much his leaving devastated her.

"Thanks," she said, casually, even though it was killing her. "Sounds great."

"Good night, Lauren." He leaned forward and brushed her mouth with his.

She clung for a brief second, trying to silently tell him with her kiss all that she dared not speak. He didn't get the message. After touching her hair, he opened the front door and disappeared into the night.

She closed it behind him, then turned the lock. And crumpled to the floor. She'd done exactly what she'd sworn not to do. Despite all the pep talks and the warning signs written in big, bold letters, she'd gone ahead and given her heart to a man who only wanted to use her.

"I love him," she whispered aloud, as the tears collected in her eyes and rolled down her cheeks. "I love him and he doesn't give a damn."

A voice inside whispered that he did care a little.

"Not enough. Not even enough to stay the night."

A few hours before, she had thought how their passion had chased away all the barriers between them. There couldn't be any more secrets. She'd been wrong. Between them stood the biggest secret of all: her love.

Why? Why had she been foolish? Why did it have to be him? There were hundreds, thousands of single men in Chicago. She'd dated several who were good-looking and successful and very interested in seeing her again. Not one of them had sparked her interest.

Was it his humor? His intelligence? What was there about Jack Baldwin that had brought her to the one place she swore she'd never be again?

She thought about calling home. Her mother would know the right thing to say. Lauren sniffed. She could use a little motherly advice. But if she called, her father would also want to talk. He'd give her his own unique advice. Soon her brothers would be threatening to rub Jack out. Better to get over the situation by herself.

Angrily she swiped at the tears on her face. Damn it, Jack wasn't worth crying over. She rose to her feet and forcefully walked to her bedroom. If he didn't want to spend the night, fine. She didn't need him in her life, or her bed. He was a hundred percent replaceable. In the morning, she'd call the Language Institute and tell them she'd be returning soon. And to think she'd been worried because the deal with Tonikita Corporation had fallen through. Jack deserved everything he had coming. And when he called to complain, she'd tell him just that. And then say, "I told you so." Victory would taste sweet.

But when she pulled back the sheets and climbed into bed, the scent of their lovemaking mocked her intentions. Without even closing her eyes, she could see his face when he reached the point of climax. She could feel his sure touch on her skin, taste the lingering sweetness of his body. She didn't have to close her eyes to remember it all. The tears blinded her and dampened her pillow long into the night.

She fell asleep sometime after five, but the ringing of the phone woke her shortly before nine.

"Hello," she said groggily, unable to focus completely.

"Lauren? It's Jack. Look, I'm sorry to wake you."

"It's okay." She blinked several times. Something about the tone of his voice wasn't right. "You sound funny. What's going on?"

"You were right."

"Jack, what are you talking about? Is everyone okay? Was there an accident?"

"I suppose that's one way of looking at it." He drew in a breath. "I got a fax from Yamashita. We've been asked to withdraw from the bidding process."

The raw pain in his voice cut through the last bits of sleep. "I'm sorry."

He paused, then said, "Me, too. I guess this is where you say, 'I told you so.' "

The sweet victory she'd promised herself. Why did it taste so bitter?

"I need to shower and get dressed," she said. "Then I'll be right over."

"You don't have to worry about picking up the pieces. I'll explain it to the team. They'll know it was my fault, not yours."

"Do you think I care about whose fault it was?"

"In your position, I would."

"I'm not you."

"Yeah. You wouldn't have blown it." He cleared

his throat. "Thanks for everything, Lauren. I know you tried to make a success of the deal, and I appreciate that. You were patient with me. I'll make it clear in your letter of recommendation that you performed perfectly."

As if he didn't have enough flaws, the man was also occasionally as thick as a post. "Are you firing me?"

"No."

"Good, because I haven't quit yet. I'll be there in an hour."

"There's no point."

"Let me decide that." She hung up without saying good-bye.

He didn't deserve her help, she thought. But he needed her, and she'd be there for him. Broken heart or not, she loved him. It wouldn't be the first time she'd been a fool for Jack Baldwin. Maybe, just maybe, it could be the last.

NINE

For once, his view of the Chicago skyline and Lake Michigan didn't please Jack. He stood at his window and stared out at the bustling city. People moved forty stories below like ants carrying invisible burdens back to their den. Cars snarled in traffic. The faint sound of a siren drifted through the glass.

He stuffed his hands into his trouser pockets. He'd come so far, he thought he'd left failure behind. That arrogance had been his downfall. He'd lost the biggest deal of his career, and he didn't have anyone to blame but himself.

For the twentieth time, he read the letter that had been faxed from Tokyo sometime in the night. The polite greeting didn't hint at the blow waiting in the next paragraph. There it was—a statement that while Baldwin International was an impressive company, its aggressively Western style of doing business didn't mesh with the more traditional philosophy at Tonikita Corporation. He had been wished well in future ventures. It was signed by Yamashita himself. Lauren had called this one, right down to the dotting of the last *i*.

He hadn't even bothered to listen when she'd tried to tell him. Turning his back on the view, he winced as he remembered her impassioned plea. Was it only yesterday? She'd told him the deal had failed, that his aggressive style had scared the Japanese company away. And he'd told her he could smell a crashed deal at fifty miles. Apparently the old skills weren't as sharp as they used to be.

The frustrating part was that he'd had every opportunity to make it a success. The tools and resources, the people and plans, had all been in place. The only problem had been him. He'd thought he could bully his way into Tonikita, the way he had with the French. Go it alone and flaunt the power, had always been his motto. Lauren had told him he'd have to change his ways to make this one fly. He hadn't listened. They would be able to see the smoke from his crash and burn for miles.

All lost. And for what? He turned his back on the window. Control. Because he had to have it his way. Because if they didn't play by his rules, he'd take his toys and go home. He'd lost it all.

He paced the length of his office, striding past the leather sofas and the wet bar tucked discreetly in one corner. It wasn't just the loss of the deal, he thought, acknowledging the guilt. He hadn't only blown it for himself and his team, he'd blown it for Lauren. She'd risked a lot to take this job. Her reputation had been on the line as much or more than his. There would be other deals for him, other places to make money. But who would give her another shot at playing in the big leagues now that her first opportunity had ended in failure? No one would care that it was all his fault. He had a track record; she didn't.

Why the hell had he hired her if he hadn't planned on listening to her? Even now he could hear her asking him the same question. He'd brushed her concerns aside. Stupidity, he thought, shaking his head. Plain male stupidity.

He'd been so caught up in playing the big boss, he'd ignored the primary rules of the game. The first of which was to remain faithful to the chase. Jack stopped in front of his desk, then collapsed in one of the two leather wing chairs. It was almost funny, he thought grimly. For years he'd joked about the chase being his mistress and that he had to be true to her. It had been his way of warning himself and women that success required focus. But he hadn't focused on this project at all. He'd spent most of his days trying to impress Lauren and the rest of them ignoring her suggestions. Hell of a way to figure out the chase *was* a jealous mistress. For the first time he'd been unfaithful, and look what had happened.

Memories from the previous night flooded him. He and Lauren had made love with the passion and heat of two reunited souls. She had given him pleasure, both in pleasing and being pleased, that far exceeded his previous experiences. It had almost been worth the price of losing. But even that had been tainted. As usual, he'd thought only of himself and keeping control. She'd wanted him to spend the night. A simple request, requiring little of him. He hadn't even been able to give her that.

So where did they go now? He owed her. Not only for the lovemaking, but for single-handedly destroying her career. The hell of it was, he had nothing to offer her in return. What could he give that would make up for what was taken, stolen really, without thought of the consequences? She was funny, intelligent, beautiful, a woman any man would be proud to claim as his own.

Jack shook his head. There he went again. *Claim.* She wasn't some prize to be won at a carnival ring toss. She was a person. The kind of woman any man would be honored to share his life with. He'd thrown her away without ever thinking he might come to regret his haste. She knew him, better than anyone. He was a predator who consumed those who got in his way. He could be tamed, perhaps, but never domesticated. And she needed someone domesticated. God knows she deserved that.

He steepled his hands and rested his chin on his fingertips. If he could do it all again . . . He couldn't of course, but the urge to relive the past consumed him. There were so many places he'd screwed up. Not just in this deal, but in others. He didn't like all this self-analysis, but he didn't know how to turn off the thoughts. That was something else Lauren had done. She'd made him take a look at himself. Had he always been a selfish bastard, or was that something new?

Someone knocked on his door.

"Go away," he called.

"The building is on fire," his secretary answered.

"Let it burn."

He heard her sigh. "I'm coming in, even if you don't want me to."

He didn't answer.

She pushed open the door. "I have some files that need signing."

He didn't bother to turn around. "You sign them. I know you've been forging my signature for years."

"Only when I had to. It won't take you but a minute."

He shook his head.

"All right, but when you find out I've doubled my salary, you'll only have yourself to blame."

He smiled for the first time since getting the letter. "You deserve it, Millie. Knock yourself out."

He heard her start to pull the door shut. There was a commotion, then a familiar voice said, "He'll see me."

Lauren.

He sprang to his feet and turned to face her. She stood just inside his office. The long hair he'd touched so much last night had been pulled into a ponytail. She wore his favorite suit, the green one that matched her eyes, and a creamy blouse that brought out the color in her cheeks. He wanted to grab her and pull her close. His own shame and the iciness in her gaze stopped him.

She stared at him for several seconds, then glanced away. He wasn't sure what to say. Then she drew in a breath and spoke.

"Do you want another chance with Tonikita Corporation?"

He couldn't have heard her correctly. "That's not possible."

"You didn't answer my question."

He ran his hand through his hair and moved around his desk to stare out the window. "Do you have to ask?"

"Yes."

There was something challenging about her this morning. He knew she was angry about last night. He wanted to apologize for walking out on her, but it wasn't the right time. He supposed that what he was feeling the most was the discomfort of failing in front of the one person he'd wanted to impress. It reminded him too much of being a powerless kid.

He shoved his hands into his pockets. "Yes, Lauren, I want another chance. Did you come here to gloat? I don't blame you. You deserve it."

"That's not why I'm here."

"Then why?"

"Look at me."

He turned slowly. She'd moved closer to his desk, and now stood behind the wing chairs.

"I can get you that chance," she said simply.

That wasn't possible. Nobody got a second chance. "How?"

"I'll call Tokyo. Yamashita owes me a favor, and he's very sensitive about his obligations."

Hope flared hot and bright inside. Jack shook his head. "As easy as that?"

She didn't smile, but the corner of her mouth twitched. "Not exactly, but you would be given another opportunity."

"Wait a minute. This doesn't wash. Weren't you the one making such a fuss when I wrote a letter telling Yamashita you were on the team, or was that another employee of mine?"

She motioned to the chair. "May I?"

"Please."

She sank into the leather seat and folded her hands on her lap. "You're right. I was opposed to being used as bait. But it was my rule, and I can break it if I want to."

"And he'd really give us another chance, based solely on your say-so?"

"Yes."

"No."

"What?"

He walked over to his chair and sat down. "I said no."

"I heard you, but why?" Green eyes darkened with confusion. "I know how much you want this, Jack. Don't let pride stand in the way."

"It's not pride."

"Then what is it?"

"Why are you helping? I would have thought that after last night, you'd be glad to see me fall on my ass."

Her gaze darted away, and a light color flared on her cheeks. "Why would you say that?"

"We both know you wanted me to stay, and I was too much the selfish bastard to bother."

"That was personal and this is business."

"Maybe," he conceded. "But you still haven't answered the question. Why are you willing to help?"

She straightened her shoulders and stiffened her spine. "My reputation is on the line here. I started this project, I want the chance to see it through."

She was lying, but he didn't know about what. And he didn't care. Second chances didn't come around often enough for him to walk away from this one. He owed his team and Lauren the opportunity to succeed. She was right; her reputation was also at stake. Hadn't he been beating himself up about that only moments before?

He leaned over his desk and pushed the phone toward her. "Make the call." Their eyes met. "Please," he added. Then he rose and left the room.

Lauren drew in a deep breath and sagged against the

back of the chair. Thank God Jack hadn't been able to see her tremble. Walking in his office this morning had been one of the hardest things she'd ever done. She'd feared what he might say to her. More than that, she'd feared exposing her heart to his ridicule. All the reasons she'd decided to come back and help him had been true, but they hadn't been complete. The last reason, and the most important, was that she loved Jack and would do anything for him. Even the one thing that would take him from her.

She had no illusions. Left alone, he might have come to her for comfort. At the very least, he would have called to apologize. Without the rules of business to be followed, the potential for a relationship had been there. Now they were back where they had been yesterday, before they had made love. He was her boss; she, his employee. Never again would his guard come down.

It was for the best, Lauren told herself. She needed this success in her professional life. When Baldwin International closed the deal—and she'd make sure they would—she'd walk away with the whole arrangement to her credit. That's what she'd wanted in the first place, she reminded herself. The chance to write her own ticket. Success was here for the taking.

And it felt so empty. She wanted Jack as much as she wanted the rest of it. Maybe more. And not just the Jack who had loved her so tenderly with his body— if not his heart—last night. She wanted the man who shocked her with his irreverence, who touched her with his thoughtful gestures, who promised to listen, then went his own way and damn the consequences.

The irony of the whole situation was that he had forced her to become just like him. There could be nothing between them now. She knew that. Once Yamashita agreed to reopen talks, Jack would once again be consumed with the deal. Lauren, the flesh-and-blood woman, would be pushed aside in favor of the chase. And in truth, *she* would give her heart and devotion to the cold financial workings of the deal.

She reached in her skirt pocket for the phone number she'd brought from home, and picked up the receiver.

The call was answered on the first ring. After identifying herself to the receptionist, she waited while Yamashita came on the line.

The sound of the old man's voice brought tears to her eyes. It had been many months since she had called him, and while she'd lived in Japan, he and his family had been an important part of her life. They chatted for several minutes about personal matters and mutual friends.

"When are you coming to visit?" he asked in Japanese.

"I don't know," she answered in the same language.

"That is not why you have called me today."

"No."

"You wish me to give Baldwin International another opportunity. Do you really believe I should? Is that company right for Tonikita? Do they know our ways? Respect our culture? Have you thought what you ask of me?"

"I do not ask lightly," she said, clutching the side of the table. "You heard about Jack Baldwin's presentation."

"Yes."

"He was not completely wrong."

Yamashita was silent for several seconds. She allowed him the time to think about what she had said. In the past, she had always approached Yamashita as a student learning from the master. This time she spoke on more equal terms. Would he allow that?

"The world is changing," he conceded.

"And you with it. Vision has always been your strength."

"And flattery yours."

She smiled into the phone. "He can help you."

"I do not need his kind of help. His ways are not ours."

"I will show him the correctness of your path."

"Why do you ask this? For the man? Or for yourself?"

This time she was the one who was silent. How much of the truth should she tell her old friend? How much would he want to know?

"I ask," she said at last, "because it is the correct thing for me to do. You may refuse me, if the wisdom of your years tells you that is the correct decision for you."

"You conveniently ignore my obligation to you."

"I have forgotten it," she lied. It's what she'd been counting on. "You should forget it as well."

Yamashita sighed. "I miss you, child. Come and see us soon."

"I promise."

"Then I will send another team to negotiate with your Jack Baldwin." He named a date. "Teach him our ways."

"I will."

"You have asked much."

"I am grateful for your indulgence."

"You have been good to my family." The older man paused. "My personal assistant will head the team this time."

Her heart dropped to the pit of her stomach. No! Anything but that! She couldn't face more humiliation. She swallowed the feeling of dread.

"Thank you for your kindness," she said, forcing out the words through stiff lips.

"They will arrive in two weeks. You must be happy to be seeing your old friend."

"I am." It was her second lie of the conversation.

They spoke for a few more minutes, then said their good-byes. Lauren wished his daughter and grandchild well, then set down the receiver.

She'd done it. Jack had his second chance. She had her second chance as well. It had been a small price to pay, she thought. Yamashita was now released from his obligation. That wasn't what was bothering her at all. It was the thought of seeing his personal assistant again. It had been years, and yet . . .

Lauren covered her face with her hands and tried to block out the memories. They were too strong and flooded her brain with pictures and words. Yamashita standing in his office, so many years ago, offering her the job of her choice. Her tearful refusal. She'd told the older man that she was going back to the States.

He'd studied her for several minutes, his dark eyes seeing past the bravado.

"You love him, don't you?"

She'd nodded, unable to speak.

"And he has chosen this other path?"

"It's better for both of us. It would never have worked."

He'd accepted those long-ago lies as easily as he'd accepted the ones she spoke today. He'd known the truth then; it wasn't foolish of her to assume he'd probably figured it out today as well.

"You could stay and fight for him," the older man had said. "Isn't that the American way?"

"She loves him, too. I can't hurt her."

Yamashita had nodded. "You are a good and loyal friend."

"She has given me a family and a place to belong. What else could I do?"

At twenty-two, she'd been convinced her heart would never heal. Yamashita had told her otherwise.

"There will be other men."

"No, there won't. But I'm still going home."

"This is your home."

She'd looked away from him. "Not anymore." After walking to the door of his office, she'd turned back. "I wish you a thousand grandsons." Then she'd fled.

When she'd settled in Chicago, he'd sent a letter reminding her of his obligation. She'd ignored it, much as she'd ignored the invitation to the wedding. Japan was too far to travel. Besides, she had no desire to watch her former lover marry her best friend. Jiro had left her for Yamashita's daughter and a guaranteed position as his assistant in Tonikita Corporation. He'd gotten a wife and success. Her share had been a broken heart and more memories than she could ever want.

She'd recovered from the broken heart, she told herself firmly. After all, she'd finally realized it had been a lot more about pride than love. She wouldn't have blindly accepted his decision if he had truly been the man for her. It was the memories that frightened her. The reminders of the past had the ability to make her feel small and inadequate, as if she'd never figure out how to fit in. Would Jiro still affect her? What would they say to each other after all this time? What if she'd been wrong and found out that she still cared about him? She couldn't let her personal feelings—or the past—upset the negotiations process. Above all, Jack must never know about her former lover.

There was a tapping on the office door. Lauren straightened in the chair and forced herself to smile.

"Come in," she called.

Jack opened the door. "Did you get through?"

He stood tall and handsome in the morning light. Dark hair tumbled over his forehead, and a slight frown drew his eyebrows together. She knew every inch of this man, had tasted him, held him, loved him with her body and her heart. She was about to face her past for him. And he would never know any of it. It was her secret. She would keep it well. This deal was her gift, an act of love. That she would benefit from it as well was inconsequential, for she would willingly have helped him without the lure of personal gain.

She rose to her feet and walked toward him. The urge to throw herself against him, to be held in those strong arms and cradled against that broad chest, quickened her pace. But when she was two feet away, she forced herself to stop. He must never know her true feelings. As much as he wanted the deal, he would turn away from her if he knew she loved him.

"We're in," she said quietly.

He blinked, his expression puzzled, as if he hadn't heard correctly. Then he swept her up in his arms and swung her around the room.

"You did it!" he said. "What a woman! You deserve a raise." Before she could do more than rest her hands on his shoulders, he lowered her to the ground and grinned. "Hot damn!"

"You're welcome," she said, smiling up at him,

forcing her hands to let go of him. "And sure, I'll take that raise."

Blue-gray eyes met hers. Fire flickered. The blue began to fade. He reached out to touch her face. She froze in place, willing him not to touch her, silently pleading with him to leave her be. His arm dropped to his side. The fire faded. The blue returned to his irises.

"So where do we begin?" he asked, stuffing his hands into his pockets.

"We have another two weeks until the new team arrives."

"New team? What are you talking about?"

"Yamashita is sending in the heavy hitters, Jack. These will be the toughest players. The head man is his personal assistant. His name is Jiro Hattori."

"Do you know him?"

She stared at Jack, not sure how to take the question. Then she realized he was asking something fairly obvious. She knew Yamashita well enough to be able to call in a personal favor. It made sense that she might know his assistant as well.

"We went to college together."

"That'll help. You'll know all his weak points."

"Anything American," she said, then wanted to call the words back. Would Jack pick up on that?

He didn't. "Terrific. I know a great steak place. We'll be sure to take them there for lunch. And maybe I'll see about tickets to a Cubs game."

"There's not going to be a lot of extra time for fun."

He glanced down at her. "Lady, there's always time for baseball."

"Oh, excuse me. I should have known."

Despite the trauma of the last twenty-four hours, she felt her spirits beginning to lift. At first she'd been concerned that Jack would be broken by the failure of the negotiations. He was always so strong; she couldn't imagine him any other way. But she'd worried for nothing. He was already back to his old self.

He placed a hand at the small of her back and ushered her to one of the wing chairs in front of his desk. As always, his touch burned clear through to her skin. She glanced up at him, but he didn't seem the least bit affected by the contact. She sighed. It was going to be a long day.

"Where do we start?" he asked, rounding the desk and pulling out his chair.

"I guess we should plan out the material to be covered. I still think your presentation itself is sound. Maybe we could make a few modifications, but nothing major."

He leaned back in his seat. "I'm the big problem."

"I wouldn't say that."

"Maybe not, but you'd think it."

She shrugged, feeling embarrassed.

"I know that in the past I didn't pay attention to what you were trying to teach me. I belittled your Zen-like calmness and did my damnedest to disrupt classes. All that is behind me, Lauren. I want this deal with Tonikita Corporation. I've never failed before and I'm not about to start now. You're the boss now. You tell me what to do and I'll do it."

The alpha male of the pack was handing her his position. She didn't want the authority, but there was no other way. If he wanted to play hardball, she would, too.

"I've heard this before," she said, staring at him.

He met her gaze head-on. "I know what I told you before. We both knew I was lying. This time—" he drew in a breath as if trying to think of a way to convince her "—I give you my word. I will listen to anything you tell me, and follow the program line by line. For the next two weeks, and through the negotiations, I am at your disposal."

Of course, their time together would end, she thought sadly. So why did he have to bring it up?

"You know this is just an invitation to see if Baldwin International and Tonikita Corporation are compatible," she said. "If you get in, there will be months more of negotiations. It could take as long as a year."

He didn't flinch. "I'm committed to this, if you are."

"I'm committed, Jack."

They were, of course, talking about completely different things. He was committed to the deal, while she . . . She sighed. It was going to be a long few weeks.

"Good. Then we're in agreement." He grinned. "If all goes well, you might have to give up your office at the Language Institute."

"Why?"

"If this is a success, I may need to offer you a permanent position."

Her heart fluttered in her chest. Don't be a fool, she told the offending organ. It didn't listen.

"Why would you do that?"

"You're a great asset to the company."

"Thanks," she said dryly, wondering if he said the same thing to his computer each morning. Her heartbeats slowed to a disappointed normal.

"Where do we start?" he asked.

"What have you told the team?"

"Nothing." He glanced at his desk, then back at

her. "It's not easy to tell people who have worked so hard for something that the boss blew it."

"Don't be so tough on yourself. Besides, they were just as excited about your presentation as you were."

"I'll have to talk to them about that. They should have known better."

"They were swept up in the moment."

"Yeah. No more sweeping."

"Fine with me."

He leaned forward and rested his elbows on the desk. "I don't deserve you, Lauren. But I'm pleased you've decided to stay on and see this through. You won't regret it."

"I'm sure it will help my career when we get Baldwin International and Tonikita together."

"You'll be a star."

A lonely star, she thought, wondering how she was going to get through the next days and weeks. It was too big a secret, but she had no choice. He could never know the truth of how she felt.

"I owe you big-time, lady," he said. The fire had returned to his eyes, stealing the color and widening his pupils. "How about dinner?"

"What about the 'business only'?"

Desire battled want; pleasure fought the deal. She knew which would win, even tried to tell herself it didn't matter. Even as he shook his head in the negative, she allowed herself to hope.

"You're right," he said ruefully. "About everything. How do you do that?"

"It's a gift." She rose to her feet. "I'm still a little rattled from all that's happened. If you don't mind, I'm going to go home. I want to figure out the best way to handle the material. Why don't I meet you back here tomorrow at eight.''

"I'll be here.'' He stood and followed her to the door. "And thanks.''

"It was nothing.''

"No. It was a helluva lot, and I'll make it up to you. After.''

"There can't be any after for us, Jack. It has to be strictly business.''

"I didn't mean today.''

"I know what you meant,'' she said sadly. "After the deal, we'll pick up where we left off last night.''

He frowned. "Don't you want to?''

Yes, her mind screamed. Tell him yes! "No,'' she said. "It would never work. We're too different and we have different priorities. I'm . . .'' Just some woman who got her heart broken, she finished silently.

"You're more than my match, Lauren Reese,'' he said sadly. He braced one hand on the closed door behind her. With his other, he touched her chin. "And you're right about this one, too. You deserve better than some old battle-weary guy like me.''

Before she could tell him that he was exactly what she needed and deserved, he leaned forward and brushed her mouth with his. The contact, as fleeting and electric as a summer storm, broke through the barrier of her resolve. A burning began behind her eyes.

"I'll always be here if you need me,'' he said, then straightened and opened the door.

Funny, she thought as she made her way down the hall. Even while he was ripping her apart inside, he continued to act like a nice guy. Why couldn't he be easy to hate?

TEN

"All right, let me see if I have this. You want the focus to be on previous long-term business relationships?" Jack asked as he stretched out on a leather couch in his office.

The drapes were wide open, allowing the late afternoon sun to shine into the room. Stacks of papers covered every available surface. Books on Japanese history and etiquette stood in piles on the floor. A tray with the remains of their lunch rested by the door, waiting to be picked up.

Lauren sat cross-legged on the center of the desk. Her large-framed glasses perched on her nose, giving her a studious air. She'd left her hair long, and while she glanced through her notes, she absentmindedly twirled a strand around her index finger.

"Exactly," she said. "You do have some, don't you?"

"Sure. There are a couple of British contracts I got the first year I joined the company."

She raised a delicate eyebrow. "Your father certainly indulged your need to play overseas."

"He'd already handed me the company. What was there to lose?" He rose to a half-sitting position. "Besides, it was for almost ten million dollars. Hardly my idea of play money."

"Tsk, tsk, we are touchy this afternoon, aren't we?"

He sighed and leaned back against the leather armrest. "*We* are going crazy from being cooped up in this room."

"It's only for the rest of today, then you get a whole weekend off."

"That's what I keep telling myself."

"Maybe it would help if you kept one thought in mind: *Deru kugi utareru.*"

"Thanks," he said, dryly. "I'll sleep better at night knowing that."

"I wasn't done."

"So you *are* going to translate?"

She rolled her eyes. "It explains the basic philosophical difference between East and West. You know the old saying about the squeaky wheel?"

"Yeah."

"The translation for the Japanese saying is 'The nail that sticks up is hit with the hammer.' "

He made a couple of notes. "Interesting. In other words, don't make waves."

"Exactly."

"Boring."

"Jack!" she said warningly. "If this contract goes through, you're going to be working with the Japanese on a regular basis. This isn't a one-time deal. If you don't like their style—"

"Yeah, yeah, I get it."

They'd been working together nonstop for almost two weeks. It was Friday. The negotiations would begin Monday morning. Jack rubbed his temples and wondered if it would be worth it. The question alone told him how tired he was. If he pulled this off, it would be the coup of the century.

He stared down at his pages of notes and bit back a groan. If he pulled this off, it would be a minor miracle.

"Okay, so I mention my ongoing relationship with the British." He scribbled on the pad. "What else?"

"Just remember what I told you about the profit angle." She slipped her glasses on top of her head. "It's not important."

"Everybody needs money to stay in business."

"We've had this discussion before."

"Yeah, and I'm still not buying your theory. You show me someone who doesn't care about making a buck, and I'll show you—"

She raised one eyebrow. "Yes?"

Damn. There he went again. He swallowed back the rest of his tirade. "A true believer," he finished lamely.

Lauren stared at him. Her mouth began to twitch. His quivered a little at the corner.

She laughed first. She tried to cover up the sound with a cough, but then another giggle escaped, and another.

"Go ahead and have fun at my expense," he said, then chuckled.

"A true believer?" she asked. "Is that the best you could do?"

"Short notice."

"Hmm. Well, you're right, in a manner of speaking.

It's not that the Japanese aren't interested in profit. Quite the contrary. But they look at it differently.''

"I know." He flipped the pages on his pad. "Here it is. My second speech discusses the need to plan for the long term. No quarterly profit reports." He winced. "The accountants are going to be out for blood."

"You can still produce them, if it makes you happy. Just don't show them around. And I thought Mike was giving that speech."

He shrugged. "I know he prepared most of the stats, but this is only his third international conference. He told me he was a little nervous, so I—" He glanced up and saw Lauren staring at him. "What?"

"Mike did a fine job last time."

"I know."

"So why are you rewarding him by taking away his moment of glory?"

Jack's temper flared. He pushed it down. She was right. He had to trust his team. But he didn't have to like it. "Fine." He made some notes. "Mike gives the talk on long-term planning." He looked at the charts pinned to the wall and swung his legs over the side of the sofa and sat up. "I've been thinking about this whole thing, and the Japanese might be on to something."

Lauren dropped her papers on the desk and clutched her heart. "Don't shock me like that. I'm not a young woman anymore."

"Can the dramatics."

She grinned. "Yes, Master. Go on. I want to hear this theory of yours."

"It's just that we spend a lot of time chasing the bottom line. In the long term, that can be a mistake.

Look at what happened with all the mergers in the late eighties.''

"I agree." She picked up her cup of coffee and sipped.

Jack watched her. Because they'd been spending most of their time camped out in his office, in the last few days they'd both taken to dressing more casually. Today Lauren wore jeans and the sweater that had driven him crazy the first time he'd visited her house. The wide neckline kept slipping over one shoulder, exposing creamy skin and her bra strap. He now knew exactly what lay beneath the knit wool and lace undergarment. He'd feasted on her breasts, teased her nipples into erect points, caressed her silken skin until she writhed beneath him in a passioned frenzy.

The office was too small to stay in this long, but where else could they go? At least here they were chaperoned, in a manner of speaking, and the team members were close by. They'd both battled bouts of going stir crazy, but the option of his place, or hers, was too dangerous. Even within the relative protection of the office, with the unspoken rule that they went home at the same time as the rest of the staff, she still got to him. Several times a day she said something or did something that aroused him. One time it had been a backward glance over her shoulder; another, it had been a slight smile, or the outline of her torso highlighted through a sheer blouse. He'd turned once and caught her adjusting her panty hose. The sight of her long legs and the gentle curve of her derriere had hardened him instantly. Yesterday he'd seen her looking at his chest, measuring the length and breadth. Her hands had clenched into tight fists and she'd turned away when their eyes had met.

The heat smoldered between them like a banked fire. It waited for a single blast of air to flame into life. So neither breathed very heavily, he thought grimly. What price victory?

He had chosen the deal over the woman. The deal, inanimate and intangible, he understood. The woman— he glanced at Lauren's bare shoulder, then away—was beyond him. Feature by feature, he could handle her. The wit, the charm, the beauty, no problem. Even her brain challenged him in a positive way. But the package taken as a whole—not for him. He didn't want, or couldn't be, what she needed. "Forever" was a concept he didn't deal with.

Love and family never crossed his mind. He'd lived his own life from the time he'd been twelve. After the death of his mother, an assortment of housekeepers had kept him in line during his infrequent visits home from boarding school. He'd learned early the value of self-sufficiency. That the only things that mattered were those he could accomplish himself. He didn't need anyone else on a permanent basis. And from all the signs, Lauren didn't play that way. So the game had been called on account of rain—or in his case, conscience.

Lauren slipped her glasses down to the bridge of her nose and picked up the papers. "If you think the accountants are going to be cranky, wait until the lawyers get ahold of the contracts."

"Assuming we're in."

"I have every confidence in you."

"I hope you're right."

"I am."

He grinned. "Are we trading places here? You're becoming the confident predator, and I'm the Zen master."

"Don't say that."

"Why?"

She shrugged. "I'm not sure I want you to be different. Not that you couldn't use a little taming, but not too much." She picked up her pencil, then set it down. "What I mean is that I never *disliked* you before."

"I don't dislike you either."

"Oh, stop teasing me." She threw the pencil at him. He ducked, and it hit the back of the sofa. "Good aim."

"I told you I was raised with two older brothers."

"Does that mean they're going to come after me if they find out we were intimate?"

"Worried about your hide, mister? The odds wouldn't be on your side. Did I mention I come from a family of burly men?"

He stretched out his feet in front of him. "Yeah, yeah, I'm really scared. Let's get back to work. We've covered the speeches, the polite inanities, the order of presentations. Is that everything?"

"No." She pulled out the schedule. "You've preempted Lorraine."

He groaned.

"Jack, this is a team effort. Why can't you trust them?"

"I do."

"Not enough to let them do their jobs."

He shook his head. "I usually work alone. I'm the one in control. I don't like loose ends."

"Let go of the control. It's the only way to succeed."

Easy for her to say, he thought, leaning his head against the back of the sofa. Control was all he had. He'd wrestled with this particular demon before. In his head, he knew she was right. But in his gut. He closed his eyes. Could he let go enough? Could he trust them? Could he trust her? Did he have a choice?

"Put Lorraine back," he said without looking at her.

"Thanks." He heard her pen scratching on paper. "Have you got your speech tape?"

"Yes." Together they'd recorded his opening speech in Japanese. He spoke aloud with the tape several times a day. "I've almost got it memorized."

"Using notes isn't a problem."

"I'm trying to impress you."

She pulled off her glasses. "Why?"

He'd meant the remark to be teasing, but it hadn't come out that way. Maybe because it was true. He *did* want to impress her. Probably because she'd seen him at his worst. He shrugged, not sure what to say.

'Jack?"

"Let it go, Lauren."

Their eyes met. The muted cream of her sweater made her eyes look even darker green. "Godzilla eyes," he murmured.

From across the room, he heard her breath catch. "I thought we weren't going to do this anymore," she said.

He almost said, "Do what?" but he knew better. The sex was safe for him. No one got hurt in bed. "You thought wrong."

"What about the deal?"

He told her in no uncertain and rather vulgar terms what the deal could do with itself.

"It's not right," she said, never looking away. The papers slipped from her hands and spilled onto the desk.

"We don't seem to be able to escape it."

"We're stronger than the passion."

"Maybe you are." He rose to his feet. "Usually when I want a woman, I take her and then it's over. With you, I want you more now than I did before. I can close my eyes and remember every inch of you. What you looked like, how you tasted and sounded. Your hands clutching at my back while I—"

"Stop!" She held up one hand. "Has it ever been about more than sex?"

"Of course. I care about you."

"For how long? Maybe until next week? Have you ever had a permanent relationship with a woman?"

"What does that have to do with anything?"

"And you're not looking for one with me?"

He tugged on the collar of his polo shirt. "What are you asking for?"

She slipped off the desk and began to gather papers together. She stood with her back to him, her shoulders stiff and squared. "More than you have available."

"Is this some sort of ultimatum? Make a commitment or all bets are off?"

"That's not fair, Jack. I never said anything about either a commitment or backing you into a corner. I just asked if you've ever had a long-term relationship before."

"I don't need them."

She turned to face him, the papers clutched in her hands like a barrier between them. "That's where we're different. I do. I can't jump in and out of your bed on command."

"Wait a minute. Are you saying I coerced you?"

"Not at all. I came to you willingly."

He didn't like the way this conversation was going. Lauren was looking for answers, and he didn't even know she'd asked any questions. What the hell had happened?

"Then what's the problem?" he asked.

"You are. You work alone, you play alone, you s-sleep alone." Her voice cracked.

"I'm sorry about that. I want to make it up to you."

"That's not the point."

"What is?"

She glanced up at the ceiling as if hoping for divine intervention. "I need more. I need a relationship to go with my sex. I need to care about someone and have him care about me. I need to know I'm more than convenient. Call me old-fashioned, but there it is. To quote you, it's my bottom line."

He didn't like the hollow feeling in his chest. The unfamiliar tension and pain made him want to hold her until she took the words back. "So it's over?"

"There's nothing to end. I work for you. I'm your employee. I'll even be your friend, but I won't be your sexual playmate."

"Lauren, don't do this."

She thrust the papers into her briefcase. "It's late, Jack, and I'm tired. I'll see you early Monday morning. Before the meeting. Try not to study too much this weekend. You wouldn't want to burn yourself out."

"You can't leave yet. I still don't understand what happened here."

She shoved her glasses into her purse and slung it over one shoulder. "That's why I have to go. This isn't about you, Jack. I guess the failing is mine. I'm sorry. I need more. I didn't realize it until today."

She walked away without looking back. He stood in the center of the room, willing her to return. After several minutes, Millie stuck her head in the door.

"I'm going home, Mr. Baldwin."

"Did Lauren leave?"

"Yes. Do you need anything else?"

"No. Good night, Millie. See you Monday."

He sounded so normal. His secretary of fifteen years didn't notice anything was wrong.

What had just happened? He had the feeling he'd been close to an answer, then she'd walked away. They hadn't fought. Had he offended her by suggesting they make love? Why the hell did every woman get so damn interested in commitment? What was so important about long-term promises? They were lies anyway. People died, or got divorced. Nothing was forever. Why pretend otherwise?

He swore out loud. He didn't need Lauren Reese. He didn't need anyone. He'd show them all he'd be fine on his own.

Lauren stood in the shower and let the hot water pour down her body. If she lived to be a thousand years old, she never wanted to experience another conversation like the one she'd had that afternoon with Jack.

If only he hadn't looked at her with passion flaring in his eyes, she might have been able to play along a little while longer. If there had been a hint that he was willing to let her inside of that wall of control. But the thought of sharing her body with him, all the while knowing her heart would be an unwelcome visitor, had made her feel empty inside. As if she would cheapen herself by giving in.

It was the nineties. Women were supposed to be able to do anything men did. It was a nice theory, but she'd never found a way to separate her body from her feelings. Sex was more than a release of tension and the momentary sharing of pleasure. For her, it was a bond. She hadn't realized it until just that afternoon. She couldn't make love with him, without reciprocated love.

It had been a big step for her to turn him down. She should be proud of herself for her strength. And she was. Sort of. As soon as the pain stopped stabbing her with every breath, she'd celebrate her empowerment. Maybe in a year she'd feel better.

After turning off the water, she pulled open the curtains and grabbed a big, peach-colored towel from the rack. Oh, Jack, she thought as she wrapped the thick cloth around her body. Why does it have to be so difficult? Why couldn't you have given in on this one?

She smiled sadly. How ironic that the very thing that made her love him would keep them apart. It was his independence and self-assurance that had drawn her in the first place. Perhaps she'd sensed something missing in her own psyche. His strength of purpose, his "go your own way and the world be damned," had rubbed off, with a less than happy ending for them both. She'd let things get out of hand, with disastrous results.

She finished drying off, then slipped on her robe. They still had the meeting with Tonikita Corporation to get through. If that was successful, months of negotiations were possible. Could she last that long, or would it be better to leave after the initial talks? Would Jack want her to stay on?

Too many questions and no answers, she thought as she walked toward her bedroom. She'd think about the future when it got around to getting here.

The phone on her nightstand rang. Jack! Was he calling to tell her he'd had a change of heart? She raced across the room and picked up the receiver.

"Hello?"

"It's been a long time. How's it hanging, babe?"

Her heart froze, then pounded into life. Her palms dampened as she clutched the slick plastic. It wasn't Jack at all. Why now? Why today? She'd always thought of herself as pretty fortunate in life's little rolls of the dice. Apparently her luck had run out.

" 'How's it hanging' is a male form of greeting and completely out of date, Jiro," she said calmly, despite the almost overwhelming urge to hang up. "I'm fine. How are you?"

Her former boyfriend chuckled. "Fine. Lonely. In town. How about dinner?"

"When did you get in?"

"This morning. I've always loved Chicago. Bright lights, terrific steaks, and the prettiest redhead this side of the— Hell, what river is it?"

"The Mississippi."

"That's right. It's been three years since my last visit to the States. I'm losing it. So how about dinner?"

"I can't."

"Other plans?"

"Yes," she lied.

"Break them."

"I can't."

"Tomorrow then. I'd hate our first meeting to be strictly business."

I'd like our first meeting to be in the year two thousand and fifty, she thought. She was torn between saying she couldn't see him, and figuring it *was* better to face the past with relative privacy. What if she said or did something stupid the first time she saw Jiro? He'd been her first boyfriend, her first lover, her first love. What if some of those feelings still lingered? Besides, she couldn't turn down the opportunity to reacquaint herself with Jiro. He was on the Tonikita team. She owed it to Jack as well as herself to do as much as she could to help Baldwin International. Even if right now she'd rather stand in front of a moving train than face Jiro in person.

"Tomorrow is fine."

He gave her the name of his hotel, and they decided on a time. When she replaced the receiver, her hand was shaking.

Without even bothering to pull back the spread, Lauren crawled onto the bed. Her whole body ached.

She closed her eyes, then opened them, not sure if she was trying to shut out the past or the present. In a matter of days, her whole life had come crashing in around her. She hadn't been prepared for any of this. Not Jack or Jiro or the meeting.

I can't, she told herself, all the while knowing she had to. It could have been so easy, she thought, if only she'd listened to the warning voice inside that had told her it was dangerous to care about Jack Baldwin.

"And then there's the property in Hawaii," Jiro said as they walked along the lakefront after their lengthy and expensive dinner. "It's a great house. You should come see it sometime."

How cozy, Lauren thought. Just you, me, and your wife. Had he already forgotten that the two women had been friends?

"Sounds lovely," she murmured, trying to be as noncommittal as possible.

"What about you?" he asked.

"Nothing much to tell. I've been at the Language

Institute. There have been a few small international jobs. This is my first big one."

He looked at her. In the glow of the streetlights along the path, his coal black hair gleamed. Dark eyes studied her face. He was, by both Eastern and Western standards, a handsome and successful man. They passed three women walking together, and all three turned to watch him go by.

His lean body topped Lauren's by several inches. Well-groomed hands held her elbow with the proper amount of respect. He'd grown up and turned into everything she'd thought he would be.

"I'm surprised you didn't make the move to the big leagues before now," he said, slipping easily into American colloquialisms.

As always, the incongruity of perfect slang coming from classic Asian features startled her. "I'm not the barracuda type, by nature."

"Still, this is America." He waved his arm to encompass the skyline. "Being a woman isn't as much of a liability."

She glanced at him sharply, but he didn't seem to notice that he'd just insulted her. Figures. Once a male chauvinist, always a male chauvinist. "It hasn't stopped me to date."

She thought about Jack and the way he treated her. He might have driven her crazy at times, but he'd never let her gender interfere with work. Okay, except for sex. She almost smiled. But it was true. Whatever problems he'd had, they'd been about the content of what she was trying to teach, and never because she was a woman. He'd given her ample room to succeed, and had expected his employees to treat her with respect.

To him, she was as qualified as he was; in some areas, more so.

"You've always been smart," Jiro said. "That's one of the things I've always liked about you."

"I know. I was, I believe, the reason you passed calculus."

"So honest. I've missed that."

He released her elbow and placed an arm along her shoulders. She stepped out of the embrace.

"How's your wife?" she asked, emphasizing the last word.

"Fine. Pregnant. Again." He snorted in disgust. "The woman's a breeding machine. All she cares about is that damn kid, and now there's going to be another one."

"I'll thank you not to refer to my godson as 'that damn kid.' "

"You're touchy tonight, aren't you? Are you suffering from a little female trouble?"

She stopped in her tracks. "All my trouble comes from men." He paused next to her. She studied his face, searching for traces of the boy she had once loved. "You've changed."

"Maybe." His smile was unconcerned. "And you've stayed exactly the same. Do the freckles still go all the way down to here?"

He drew his finger from her throat down toward her breasts. She smacked his hand away. What a jerk!

The revelation was so startling, she laughed out loud. My God, all these years, she'd been mourning the loss of a jerk.

"What's so funny?" he asked.

"You." She laughed again. "I was wrong. You

haven't changed. I'm the one who's different. Why did Yamashita send you?''

"What do you mean?"

The pieces of the puzzle were clicking into place. Yamashita had never been happy with his daughter's choice of a husband. And the position of assistant to the president, while sounding good, didn't actually involve a lot of power.

"Why were you sent?" she asked.

Jiro shrugged. "To head the team."

"I don't buy it. You might be the figurehead, but you don't have any influence. Maybe it's a test, or he just wants to get you out of his hair for a while."

He flushed. A couple walked past them, forcing Lauren and Jiro to crowd together on the side of the path.

"How dare you," he said through clenched teeth. "You can't insult me."

She was about to tell him she already had, but she held the thought in. No sense in putting all her cards on the table. To borrow from her lessons with Jack, sometimes playing along with the game meant being in control.

She'd bet money that Watanabe was going to be there Monday morning. He'd really liked what Jack had to say at the first meeting. Jiro might be seated in the most honored chair, but Watanabe had the power. She fought a grin. Her former mentor had nearly fooled her.

Nodding her head in a show of submission, she said, "Forgive me, Jiro. I spoke out of turn."

He forced his tight features to relax into a pleasant smile. "I accept your apology. Let's not spoil our evening with all this talk about business. I've got a penthouse suite with a view that will knock your socks off. Let's go have a look."

He took her arm, but she pulled free. "No."

"No? Lauren, it's been years. How can you refuse?"

His arrogance shouldn't have surprised her, but it did. Zen calm in business was one thing, but in her personal life she'd learned to be strictly Western.

"You mean because I was once a fool for you?" she asked. "Grow up, Jiro. I did. Come Monday morning I'm going to nail your ass, and show you exactly how the pros do it."

His eyebrows drew together. "Bitch!"

"You might be able to scare your traditional wife but I'm a different sort of woman. I don't have time for you anymore." She started to walk away, then paused and looked back at him. "Oh, and Jiro, if you screw this up for me, I'll call Yamashita and tell him about your invitation to join you in your suite."

"He'd never believe you," he said, dismissing her with a flick of his hand.

"You want to test that theory? There's a public phone." She pointed to the glass and metal kiosk. When he didn't respond, she laughed and walked away.

Jack cranked up the CD player, then settled back in the chair. He didn't usually listen to country music, but tonight it spoke directly to his soul. It was dark in the room. The moon shone through the floor-to-ceiling windows, providing the only illumination.

As the singer went on about how the whiskey wasn't getting the job done anymore, Jack raised his half-full glass in salute.

"Got that right, buddy," he said, then took another sip. It was his third in less than an hour. The hell o it was, he was still stone-sober and hurting worse than a gut-shot dog.

He hadn't slept the night before. Echoes of his conversation with Lauren had filled the room until he'd wanted to scream for silence. The memories wouldn't leave him alone. He'd remembered spending his twelfth Christmas alone, even after his father had promised to come home. "It's business, son," the older man had said. Jack had tried to understand, but it had been his first holiday after the death of his mother. He'd learned quickly that business and himself were the only things he could count on. He'd graduated Summa Cum Laude with his M.B.A. and had never looked back. The deal had been faithful to him for years. So why did a future alone feel so bleak?

Neither the song nor the liquor provided an answer. It was late. He should try to sleep, even if it seemed impossible. He flipped off the music and started across the room. The ringing of the phone halted him in his tracks.

"Hello?" he said into the receiver.

"Jack, it's Lauren. I'm sorry to call so late. I hope I didn't wake you."

Her soft voice caught him like a sucker punch to the gut. All the air left his lungs. He had to inhale sharply before he could speak. "I wasn't asleep."

"Good. I found out a couple of things tonight. I wanted to run them by you. Do you have the list of the team members with you?"

"What?" She wanted to talk about business? He groaned silently with pain and frustration. He'd created a monster. "The list. I guess, yeah. Why?"

"Could you get it?"

"Hold on." He set his drink and the receiver down,

then reached for the briefcase he'd brought home the previous day. After snapping on a floor lamp, he picked up the phone and spoke. "I've got it here. What's going on?"

"Are you all right?" she asked. "You sound funny. Are you sure I didn't wake you?"

"I wasn't sleeping."

"Are you drunk?"

The outrage in her voice made him smile. "No, but not for lack of trying." There was silence. "Lauren, are you still there?"

"I never wanted to hurt you."

"I know. You didn't." He hadn't meant the statement as a lie, and it shocked him to find out it was. How could she hurt him if he didn't care about her? "What did you want to talk about?"

"Is Watanabe listed as a team member?"

Jack scanned the list. "Yeah. He's number two after that Jiro character."

"That's what I thought."

The liquor must have finally started to work, because he didn't have a clue as to what she was talking about. "You want to share those thoughts with your boss?"

"What? Oh, sure. I had, ah, dinner with Jiro tonight."

"And?"

"Well, something happened." Her voice sounded funny.

The knot in Jack's stomach tightened. "What kind of something? Did he make a pass at you?"

Silence.

"Damn it, Lauren. He did, didn't he? I'll beat the crap out of him on Monday. Hell, tell me what hotel he's staying in and I'll do it tonight."

She sighed. "He didn't make a pass at me. I was just surprised by the question, is all."

He cursed under his breath. His brain was getting fuzzier by the second. He couldn't tell if she was lying or not. His instincts said yes, but around her, his batting average on intuition was about zero.

"So what happened, then?"

"Nothing really specific, it was more of a feeling."

"You called because you had a feeling?"

"It's a very strong one."

"Terrific." He sank on the couch and placed the phone on his stomach. Cradling the receiver between his ear and his shoulder, he rubbed his aching temples. "And this feeling was . . ."

"I think Jiro is a front, and Watanabe is the real power broker."

"Why?"

"He was here before. You and he got along well. Of all Yamashita's people, he's the most progressive. Tonikita Corporation is well behind the times with their continued obedience to the old school, and if they want to keep up globally, they're going to have to change. I think that had as much to do with the decision to give us another chance as my phone call."

Us. She'd said *us.* It didn't mean anything, he told himself. But it sounded great.

"So you think that on some level they know Baldwin International is a good match for them?"

"Yes. My guess is that they're hoping to find a progressive company that can help them move forward. If we can tone down enough so that they feel comfortable working with us, they'll sign on."

"I hope your feeling is right."

"Me, too."

He closed his eyes and pictured her on the other end of the phone. What was she wearing? Jeans? A robe? Nothing? The last picture caused an instant hardening in his groin. He could see her sitting on the edge of her sofa, her knees pulled up to her chest, her long hair tumbling around her shoulders.

The silence between them continued. The sound of her soft breathing soothed him.

At last she spoke. "Jack, it's late. I should let you get some sleep."

Fat chance. "Sure. No problem." Say good-bye, he told himself, but he didn't want to let her go. "Lauren?"

"Yes."

"I'm sorry."

"Don't be."

He smiled, then reached up and clicked off the lamp. He liked being alone with her in the dark. "You don't know why I'm apologizing."

"Okay, what are you sorry about?"

"For not spending the night. I would have, except I wanted to."

"What? That doesn't make sense."

"It does to me. I don't usually spend the night. I have a couple of times because it was easier than creating a scene. I knew you wanted me to, and I wanted to stay. That's why I had to leave. And I'm sorry."

"I understand."

He sighed. "I wish I did."

"You're a good man, Jack Baldwin. Maybe you should give yourself a break."

"I didn't mean to let you down."

"You didn't," she whispered. "From the beginning I've known what would happen between us."

"Then why did you make love with me?"

"Because I had to know what it was like to be with you."

"Was it worth it?"

She paused.

He held his breath and wondered why he'd set himself up. If she said no, he'd have to crawl into the corner and whimper until the pain killed him.

"Yes, Jack. It was worth it. All of it. I can't regret knowing you."

Her honesty hurt almost as much as the expected rejection. Damn, this emotional stuff was a bitch. He clutched the receiver. "I wish I could have been what you needed, Lauren. I wish I could believe like you do in forevers or happy endings or whatever it is."

"I guess it all comes down to trusting someone to love you, Jack. Either you do or you don't. Wishing doesn't make it so. Good night."

Before he could speak, she hung up the phone.

Love? He stared at the receiver. Had she said *love?* As in "I love you"? No. No way. Not her. Not him. She couldn't love him. No one had. Women had wanted him. Hell, a couple had even proposed. But love? Never.

He walked over to the CD player and hit the start button. As the strains of the song filled the room, he poured another three fingers of scotch into his glass, then returned to the couch. It was going to be another long night.

ELEVEN

"How did it go?" Sally asked.

Lauren set her gym bag and racquet on her assistant's desk and grinned. "Excellent. I scored ten points in my best game."

"Wow. Those lessons are paying off. Another couple of months and you'll be able to beat him."

Her smile faded. She wouldn't be around in a couple of months. "I hope you're right," she said quickly, and escaped into her office.

What she didn't tell her assistant was that the reason she'd done so well playing racquetball was that Jack had obviously not slept in almost three days. There had been dark circles under his eyes, and a lack of energy in his normally disgustingly alert play.

At first she hadn't been sure he'd even show up for the game, and had wondered if she should either. But they'd been meeting every Monday, Wednesday, and Friday morning for over a month, so she'd gone to the club, just in case. He'd been waiting.

For once, the hour of exercise had been silent, except for the thumping of the ball against the floor and the wall, and the statements about serving and points. No easy banter had stirred her wit, no stolen glances had excited her body. There had been no casual contact as the ball was exchanged. He'd been strictly business; make that strictly racquetball. It was as if she'd hurt him by her declaration last week. But how could she hurt a man who didn't care about her?

Oh, she knew he liked her, but there wasn't any love involved, or even anything close. So what was wrong? She opened the armoire next to the window and stored her athletic gear. Maybe he'd figured out that she loved him, and he was embarrassed to be around her. Then why would he bother showing up for her game? She sighed. It was all too confusing. The only thing she could afford to think about was the meeting with Tonikita Corporation. She glanced at her watch. Thirty minutes until it started all over again.

By the time she'd gone over her notes, she could hear the team assembling in the hall. Someone knocked on her door.

"Come in," she called.

Jack stuck his head in. "Ready?"

She rose to her feet and gathered her papers together. "Sure. You look much better."

"Think so?" He rubbed his freshly shaved face and grinned. "I spent about fifteen minutes in the whirlpool. I think it made me a new man."

His blue-gray eyes met hers. Nothing in his gaze hinted at any pain. Had she been wrong?

"I didn't get a lot of sleep this weekend," he said, as if he could read her mind. "I was going over the notes I'd written up. I wanted to let you know I've made a few changes.''

Oh God. It was happening again. She moved toward him.

"Hey.'' He stepped into the room. The black suit he wore hugged his body with an appeal that could only be created by honest muscle and superior tailoring. "Don't panic. I'm talking about modifications, not new plays. We're going to win this time.'' He leaned forward and cupped her chin. The warm touch threatened to melt her bones. "I promise.''

"Okay.'' She reached up and stroked the back of his hand. He was warm and alive and the only man she had ever loved. Jiro had been a mistake brought on by loneliness and location. Jack might be galaxies away from her in style and direction, but underneath, they were soul mates. It hurt so much to know she'd never had a chance. "I wish—''

"Don't.'' He covered her lips with his fingers. "Don't say anything. We've got these couple of weeks to get through, then we'll renegotiate. Don't make any hasty plans.''

She jerked her chin free. "I can't continue to work for you, Jack.''

His eyes darkened, but with sadness rather than passion. "I know.''

His admission startled her. She hadn't expected him to give up without a fight. Then she reminded herself they weren't fighting for the same thing.

Before she could respond, a thin young man with curly blond hair and glasses stepped into her office.

"Ah, hi, Lauren, Jack.'' Mike pushed up his glasses and smiled nervously. "I wanted to talk about the speech on long-term planning. Maybe it would be better if you gave it, Jack. You have more experience, and, well, you'd be more comfortable talking with the Japanese.''

Lauren held her breath. What would Jack say? She knew how hard it had been for him gradually to let go of the control of this project. With the French, he'd worked alone. Over the last couple of weeks he'd become part of a team.

Jack patted the younger man on the back. ''You know those statistics better than anyone, kid. You prepared the report, you give the presentation. You're the best person for the job.''

Mike practically glowed. ''Thanks, Jack. I won't let you down.'' He turned and left the room.

''Don't say a word,'' Jack growled to her.

Lauren thought about telling Jack how much she admired him. She thought about telling him he was already changing and maybe she could chance sticking around. She thought about telling him she loved him. But it wasn't the time. Instead she took his arm and stepped toward the meeting room.

''Let's go make a killing,'' she said.

As before, Lauren led the Japanese businessmen up to the conference room. Jack hung back observing them, wondering if her take on the situation was correct. Had Watanabe been sent back as a ringer? Was that Jiro guy just a front? Interesting possibilities.

He watched Jiro Hattori move confidently through the room. The handsome younger man spoke English perfectly. Not only was his accent American, but he'd mastered most of the slang. Sally was entranced. Lauren's assistant practically swooned as she hung on the man's every word.

Lauren excused herself from another group and pulled her assistant away from Jiro. Jack frowned. That didn't make sense. Why would Lauren care if the two got along? She wasn't the jealous type. As he continued to study the trio, he noticed Jiro's gaze continually moved up and down over Lauren's body. There was a possessiveness to the perusal, as if he knew exactly what was underneath her conservative boxy suit. Lauren caught Jiro in the act and gave him a warning glare. The Japanese man stiffened slightly, then tried to cover his discomfort with a smile.

The pieces of the puzzle suddenly clicked into place. Jack remembered Lauren's hesitation when he'd asked if she'd known Jiro back in Japan. He recalled that she'd had dinner with the other man Saturday night and had been surprised when he'd asked about Jiro making a pass at her. Jiro wasn't just an old friend at all.

Jack moved through the crowd until he reached Lauren. He nodded to her assistant. "Excuse us, Sally," he said, pulling Lauren with him and out into the hallway.

"What's wrong?" she asked.

He waited until he closed the conference room door before speaking. "You should have told me."

"What?"

"That you knew Jiro before."

"I told you I did."

"Not that you knew him intimately."

Her eyes snapped. "It was a long time ago."

"Not long enough. I saw the way he was looking at you."

"He's a jerk, and it's none of your business."

Jack tightened his hands into fists. "I may not be a samurai warrior, lady, but I'm the best that you've got.

I'm going to beat the crap out of that guy, and it's going to feel great.'' He moved toward the door.

"Jack, you can't!"

"Watch me." He put his hand on the doorknob.

"Wait!" She clutched his arm. "You'll ruin everything."

"I don't give a damn. He hurt you."

"Years ago."

"And made a pass at you."

"I took care of that."

"How?"

"I threatened to tell Yamashita."

"So?"

"If you promise not to run in there like some caveman, I'll tell you everything."

He glanced at his watch. "You have one minute to convince me not to draw blood."

"Jiro and I were lovers in college."

The bald statement landed on his gut and forced the air from his lungs. He leaned against the wall and tried to breathe. "And," he managed hoarsely.

"My best friend fell for him, too. Our last year in college, he decided she was more politically correct for him than I was."

"Why?"

Lauren shrugged. "She's Japanese."

"And?"

"And Yamashita's daughter. Jiro's future was guaranteed."

Jack whistled softly. "So he's an asshole *and* he broke your heart."

"Something like that. There's more."

"So far, I'm not convinced he doesn't deserve a beating, but go on."

"What upset me the most is that he wanted me to be his mistress. I could have gotten a job in Japan. Then he would have had both the job he wanted, and his American girlfriend on the side."

If the last verbal blow had left him winded, this one left him dazed. He wasn't a rocket scientist, but even he could read between the lines. "You loved him, and he wouldn't give you any kind of permanent commitment."

She stared over his shoulder. "It was a long time ago."

"Not long enough."

"Promise me you won't beat him up."

He clenched and unclenched his fists. "I'll think about it. But if he makes one wrong move toward you—"

"He won't. Jerk or not, Jiro is a coward."

Jack forced himself to relax. He leaned forward. "Look, Lauren, I don't know if this is the time or the place, but—"

The door opened. Sally stuck her head out. "You guys going to talk all day, or are we going to get this meeting under way?"

Jack nodded. "We'll be right there. This will keep."

Lauren glanced up at him. Her green eyes begged him to finish what he'd been about to say. He wanted to tell her the truth: He was changing. Things were different then they had been just a few days ago. She was a part of the change, but he didn't know what it all meant. He needed the reprieve and some time to figure things out.

One thing was clear, however. He couldn't afford to lose her. But was he capable of what it would take to keep her?

* * *

"Interesting point, Jack," Mr. Watanabe said, leaning back in his chair. "I wouldn't have thought long-term planning was your company's strong suit."

Lauren held her breath. It was the second week of the meetings. For the first five days, the two teams had exchanged presentations and discussed general concepts. Since late Monday, however, the tone had changed. Watanabe and Jack were involved in an elaborate game of cat and mouse. The older man seemed to fluctuate between a sharing, conciliatory attitude and a "show me what you can do" stance. So far, Jack had kept his wits and his temper. It was now Wednesday afternoon. How much longer would this go on?

"You've already heard Mike's presentation on the subject." Jack smiled at his employee, then picked up a pen. "As a company and a team, we see advantages in both long- and short-term planning," he said calmly. "One has to be able to plan for the future while maintaining a position that allows one flexibility in a changing market."

The older man nodded to concede the point. "So you have had long-term relationships with your other foreign partners?"

"Yes. Baldwin International has had an ongoing joint venture with the British for over twelve years."

He continued speaking. Lauren sipped her water and tried to maintain her cool. Why was Watanabe playing this game? Was it Yamashita's doing? She wouldn't put it past her old friend to have something up his sleeve. Jiro had given up all pretense of being the leader sometime last week. She didn't know if Jack had actually said something to the other man, but somewhere in the middle of negotiations, her former lover had become quite apologetic. Currently he was doing his best to give her a wide berth.

She glanced over at Jack. He'd abandoned his suit jacket sometime after lunch. Even as he spoke, he absentmindedly rolled up the sleeves of his white shirt. She loved watching his long fingers work at any task. The natural grace inherent in his movements never failed to send a ripple of desire shooting through her. She'd love him forever. She'd want him even longer. This situation between them was going to rip her heart out and leave her gasping for life. And she couldn't find it within her to say she was sorry. Whatever the price, it was worth it to have belonged to Jack, if only for a night.

"I like what you're saying," Watanabe said.

Lauren bit back a smile as she thought the older man had been spending too much time with Jiro.

"I'm glad," Jack answered.

"But," his opponent went on, "we are not the British."

Jack glanced at his notes, then closed the folder. Instinctively Lauren tensed. Then she forced herself to relax. In the last seven days of meetings, he hadn't once done anything to jeopardize the deal. He'd learned his lesson well. She owed him her trust.

"You're right," he said. "You're not the British, and Baldwin International isn't your first choice for a partner. But it's a lot like baseball. A good hitter usually hits best on his home field. But when he's away, he's still a damn fine hitter. Trades are often made for the good of the team. Not everybody's happy about them, but they learn to get along."

Watanabe raised one eyebrow. "The Cubs lost on Saturday."

"They won Sunday."

"So the two games were a wash."

Jack grinned. "Not for the people who only had tickets on Saturday."

The man from Japan chuckled. "Tell me, Jack, what do you think of Tonikita Corporation?"

"I think it's a fine organization with a strong management team." He glanced at Jiro, then at Lauren. "With a wily man leading the show."

"You have learned many of our ways. Are we capable of learning yours?"

"You're no fool."

"I could say the same." The older man rose to his feet. "I have a flight back to Japan this evening. We will be in touch." He walked around the table and offered Jack his hand.

Lauren stood and blinked. The quick resolution had caught her off guard. She knew she'd been daydreaming about Jack's body and the way it made hers feel. Stupid, she thought. She'd missed something vital. But what?

The rest of the good-byes were made quickly. When the Japanese team had left, Jack turned to Lauren. "Well?"

"I don't know."

"Me, either. New, huh?" He offered his employees a grin. "You all did a fine job. Take tomorrow off. The soonest we'll hear is Tuesday. Maybe it won't even be until next week. Whatever the outcome, I'm proud of your efforts on the company's behalf. Thanks."

They moved toward the door, then paused as one, turned, and applauded him. Lauren saw the pleasure flare in his eyes. She clapped, too. He had performed magnificently.

"I'm impressed," she said, when the last of the team had left the room and closed the door, leaving her and Jack alone.

He leaned against the corner of the desk. "Don't be. I couldn't have done it without you."

"It was your decision to try again, and your hard work that made the success possible."

"And teamwork. Are we in?"

She shook her head and pushed herself up onto the desk. Their shoulders brushed. "I wasn't kidding about not knowing. I couldn't read Watanabe. I think that's a good sign."

"There's nothing to do but wait." He folded his arms over his chest. "Even if they okay the negotiations, you're going to be leaving."

He wasn't asking a question, but she answered anyway. "Yes."

"And if I ask you to stay?"

She saw the hurt and confusion in his eyes. It would be so easy to give in; the price was her self-worth. She couldn't afford the payment. "Please don't."

He draped his arm over her shoulders and urged her to lean on him. Slowly she lowered her head until she rested against him. It hurt so much to touch like this. The warmth of his body invaded her skin. Like a silent marauder, it crept through her pores and attacked nerve endings. His long fingers massaged her scalp.

"I love your hair," he said, then kissed the top of her head. "I love the way it shines in the light. I love the colors. I love that it used to make you feel awkward, because those years in Japan keep you from believing you're beautiful."

"Jack?" She glanced up at him. "I can't do this."

"No one is asking you to. Have dinner with me tonight."

She started to refuse, but he touched her lips with his fingers.

"Have dinner with me. To say good-bye."

The rush of tears surprised her. She blinked to hold them back.

Good-bye. It sounded so final. She'd thought about being apart, but not the actual leaving. Could she see him one more time? Could she not?

"Just dinner," he said. "In a very public restaurant. I promise."

How disappointing. Even to the end, he was going to be a nice guy.

"I'd like that."

"Good. My place, say, seven."

"Your place?" She scrambled off the desk.

"It's closer to the restaurant. Besides, I didn't think you'd want me back at your house."

"Oh. Sorry. Sure, I'll be there at seven."

He wrote the address on a sheet of paper and handed it to her. "We have a lot to talk about. Don't be late."

What on earth did they have to talk about? she wondered for the thousandth time. The elevator moved swiftly toward the penthouse.

Jack's condo was in one of those high-rise buildings along the lake. Once she'd given her name, the doorman had ushered her right through. As the elevator soared up toward the top, she found herself battling hope and expectation. She wanted him to say something wonderful that would allow her to stay both with the company and with him. It wasn't going to happen. She'd already told him the truth: Wishing someone loved you didn't make it so. Even the hungriest wolf eventually realized there were certain prey that couldn't be caught.

The double doors slid open. Lauren stepped into the foyer. There were only two doors on the top floor, and one of them stood partially open. She walked up and knocked before entering.

"Jack?"

"I'm in the kitchen. Come on in."

She shut the door behind her, turned, and gasped. One entire wall was floor-to-ceiling windows. Dusk approached, and the lights of the city were beginning to twinkle in the twilight.

She walked to the glass. It was like a magic mirror, she thought. If she strained hard enough, she could see forever.

"Impressive, huh?" he asked as he walked into the living room.

She turned and smiled. "Wonderful. How do you ever sleep? I'd want to look out at this all the time."

"You get used to it." He handed her a glass of white wine. He kept his arm raised as if he were going to touch her, then lowered it to his side. "You look pretty."

"Thanks." She glanced down at her pale peach cocktail dress, then at his jeans and polo shirt. "But we appear to be operating under different dress codes. I take it the restaurant is casual?"

"Very." With the sweep of his arm, he indicated past the living room to an elevated dining area. The black lacquered table had been set for two.

"You promised me a restaurant."

"I lied." There was nothing contrite about his smile. What else had he lied about? She ought to march right out of here and drive back to her place. Instead, she sat on the edge of his sofa and took a sip of wine. When she gathered the tattered shreds of her composure around her shoulders, she glanced up at him.

"Don't think this means you've won."

The smile faded. "I don't."

With that, he moved to the Queen Anne chair opposite the couch. Someone, probably a well-paid decorator, had turned his place into a showpiece. Old and new blended together in quiet elegance. The dining room was pure modern, with lacquered furniture and bold geometric paintings. In the living area, an antique armoire held the latest stereo equipment, while the bucket holding wood beside the fireplace looked early American.

She sat her drink on a coaster on the carved coffee table. "Why have you lured me here?"

"I'll be damned if I know. I had this plan. . . ." He shook his head. "Dumb."

His red polo shirt brought out the tan in his skin. He'd shaved recently. She missed the dark stubble defining the clean line of his jaw and the hollows in his cheeks. She missed his dimple when he wasn't smiling, like now. Okay, she'd admit it. She hadn't even left, and she already missed him. She took another drink of wine.

"I grew up here in Chicago," Jack said, resting his ankle on the opposite knee. "With the rich folks. My mom died when I was a kid."

She nodded. "You told me that. You must have missed her a lot."

"Yeah. Dad traveled on business. I didn't have any brothers or sisters, so I learned pretty quick that the only person I could count on was me. By controlling the situation as much as I could, I made it all hurt less.''

Dark brows drew together. The fleeting sign of pain made her want to go to him and offer comfort. She couldn't. Comfort would lead to passion. She had to stay strong. She owed it to herself—and to Jack. They'd both be damaged by another brief encounter.

''You can't control people,'' she said.

'You can shut them out. Give them enough on the surface so they're interested, but never let them in here.'' He touched his chest. ''Maybe it started as a defense mechanism. All I know is that it worked just fine. I got what I wanted.''

''Including women.''

Their eyes met. ''Lots of women. I don't want there to be any secrets between us, Lauren. With the problems out there today . . .'' He glanced out the window, then back at her. ''I haven't been stupid, but before that, I never lacked for female companionship. I liked women and they always liked me.''

A lump formed in her stomach. She knew there was a reason she'd never been overly fond of the honesty movement. It hurt!

''But they never loved me.''

That got her attention. ''What?''

''There's a difference between love and want.''

''I know, but—''

''No buts. It's true. I could give them position, money, a good time in bed. A few tried to force a commitment, but I waited them out. They all left, or would have if I hadn't left first.''

Including me, she thought, and had a horrible sinking feeling. Was she making a mistake?

''The point is, Lauren, I never cared about them. I

never . . ." He rose to his feet and walked toward the window. When he reached the large pane of glass, he turned and stuffed his hands into his jeans pockets. "I never loved them. I didn't know how. I didn't know what they were talking about when they said they wanted a commitment. Forever is a tough concept for me."

Her palms grew damp. She rubbed her hands together. "What are you saying?"

He moved closer, stopping about two feet in front of her. "I was going to offer you a big raise to stay. Even some shares of the company. A different office, more staff."

"It wouldn't work."

"I figured that out on my own. So I tried to think of what I could give you that you didn't have. Not a place to live." He glanced around the room. "I like your house better. Not money, not position, not power."

People talked about hope as if it were an elusive bird that showed up from time to time, then disappeared for years on end. Lauren found hope to be an undying kernel that insisted on sprouting to life at the most inopportune times. It blossomed inside of her, and thrust out in all directions. She could barely breathe for the hope pressing against her ribs.

Oh, please, she prayed.

He pulled his hands out of his pockets and squatted down in front of her.

"I finally came up with this," he said, then placed a diamond solitaire ring into the palm of her hand and closed her fingers around it. She felt the gold band, warm from his body, and the sharp edges of the cut stone. "Like I said, I don't understand about commitments and forever. So I'll promise you something else instead. I promise to love you for as long as I'm able to draw breath. I'll treat you with respect. I'll cherish your body. I promise to listen and learn to the best of my ability and not try to control you or the situation. I promise to be an equal partner in raising our children. I want to marry you, if you'll have me.''

The tears flowed fast and furious down her face. She tried to speak, but no words came.

"Why are you crying?" he asked, puzzled. One finger touched the moist trail. "I thought you'd be happy."

"I am," she managed at last. "I love you."

He smiled then, the megawatt grin that melted her bones. "I figured that out, too."

EPILOGUE

It was a small wedding, attended mostly by friends and family. Lauren's father, the general, was there, as were her mother and the two burly brothers.

Kiyoshi Yamashita had flown in from Japan to attend the wedding of the godmother of his firstborn grandson. The patriarch had a seat of honor at the front of the church.

"When you return from your honeymoon, we will begin working out the details of the joint venture," the old man said as he adjusted the cuffs of his suit.

Jack cleared his throat and tried not to act nervous. The church was filling up quickly. How many people had Lauren invited?

"We'll have to work fast," he told Yamashita. "Lauren's going to be pregnant by the time we get back, and she doesn't want to work with a newborn."

The old man raised his eyebrows. "You have *decided* she will be pregnant?"

"Of course. What's the problem?"

The old man laughed. "You have fooled us all, Jack Baldwin. Lauren promised me you had reformed your ways, but I see you are still the wolf at heart."

Jack shook his head. "I'm just a domesticated lapdog now."

The minister came in from the side of the church and motioned for Jack to take his place. Organ music began playing.

Jack clasped his hands behind his back and waited impatiently through the parade of attendants. At last, when he knew his heart was about to leap from his chest, the music swelled and a vision in white appeared at the end of the aisle.

She moved toward him, dressed in lace and satin, with mahogany hair tumbling over her shoulders. He didn't know what he'd done to deserve her, but he wasn't going to ask any questions.

Lauren's father handed over the bride.

"Hi," he whispered, squeezing her fingers. "You're the most beautiful woman I've ever seen."

"You don't get out much," she teased. Her skin glowed as if touched with candlelight, and the love in her eyes made his own burn.

"Enough." He adjusted the collar of his tuxedo shirt.

"You hate all this, don't you?"

"I'd have been happy with some civil ceremony and then several days of making love in the sun."

"You gave me the wedding, I'm giving you Hawaii."

"Fair enough."

She smiled impishly. "Did I tell you Jiro offered us the use of his house?"

Jack's answer was a growl. "Yes. We're staying in

a hotel that has room service, and I'm not letting you out of my bed for at least a week."

"I thought you wanted to make love on the sand."

He touched her cheek. "That's for the second week."

"Excuse me," the minister said, leaning forward. "Did you two want to get married, or would you rather chat a little longer?"

"Oh." Jack glanced over his shoulder at the amused congregation. "I guess we can get married."

"Wait," Lauren said, then raised herself up on tiptoes and brushed her lips against his. "I love you, Jack Baldwin."

"I thought the kiss came later," he said.

"It does," she said.

"Then what was that for?"

"For luck."

He touched her cheek. "I can't get any luckier than this."

SHARE THE FUN . . .
SHARE YOUR NEW-FOUND TREASURE!!

You don't want to let your new books out of your sight?
That's okay. Your friends can get their own. Order below.

No. 91 FIRST MATE by Susan Macias
It only takes a minute for Mac to see that Amy isn't so little anymore.

No. 159 MASTER OF THE CHASE by Susan Macias
Jack is used to getting whatever he wants. Lauren has rules of her own.

No. 90 HOLD BACK THE NIGHT by Sandra Steffen
Shane is a man with a mission and ready for anything . . . except Starr.

No. 92 TO LOVE AGAIN by Dana Lynn Hites
Cord thought just one kiss would be enough. But Honey proved him wrong!

No. 93 NO LIMIT TO LOVE by Kate Freiman
Lisa was called the "little boss" and Bruiser didn't like it one bit!

No. 94 SPECIAL EFFECTS by Jo Leigh
Catlin wouldn't fall for any tricks from Luke, the master of illusion.

No. 96 THERE IS A SEASON by Phyllis Houseman
The heat of the volcano rivaled the passion between Joshua and Beth.

No. 97 THE STILLMAN CURSE by Peggy Morse
Leandra thought revenge would be sweet. Todd had sweeter things in mind.

No. 98 BABY MAKES FIVE by Lacey Dancer
Cait could say 'no' to his business offer but not to Robert, the man.

No. 99 MOON SHOWERS by Laura Phillips
Both Sam and the historic Missouri home quickly won Hilary's heart.

No. 100 GARDEN OF FANTASY by Karen Rose Smith
If Beth wasn't careful, she'd fall into the arms of her enemy, Nash.

No. 101 HEARTSONG by Judi Lind
From the beginning, Matt knew Lainie wasn't a run-of-the-mill guest.

No. 102 SWEPT AWAY by Cay David
Sam was insufferable . . . and the most irresistible man Charlotte ever met.

No. 103 FOR THE THRILL by Janis Reams Hudson
Maggie hates cowboys, *all* cowboys! Alex has his work cut out for him.

No. 104 SWEET HARVEST by Lisa Ann Verge
Amanda never mixes business with pleasure but Garrick has other ideas.

No. 105 SARA'S FAMILY by Ann Justice
Harrison always gets his own way . . . until he meets stubborn Sara.

No. 106 TRAVELIN' MAN by Lois Faye Dyer
Josh needs a temporary bride. The ruse is over, can he let her go?

No. 107 STOLEN KISSES by Sally Falcon
In Jessie's search for Mr. Right, Trevor was definitely a wrong turn!

No. 108 IN YOUR DREAMS by Lynn Bulock
Meg's dreams become reality when Alex reappears in her peaceful life.

No. 109 HONOR'S PROMISE by Sharon Sala
Once Honor gave her word to Trace, there would be no turning back.

No. 110 BEGINNINGS by Laura Phillips
Abby had her future completely mapped out—until Matt showed up.

No. 111 CALIFORNIA MAN by Carole Dean
Quinn had the Midas touch in business but Emily was another story.

No. 112 MAD HATTER by Georgia Helm
Sara returns home and is about to make a deal with the man called Devil!

No. 113 I'LL BE HOME by Judy Christenberry
It's the holidays and Lisa and Ryan exchange the greatest gift of all.

Meteor Publishing Corporation
Dept. 793, P. O. Box 41820, Philadelphia, PA 19101-9828

Please send the books I've indicated below. Check or money order (U.S. Dollars only)—no cash, stamps or C.O.D.s (PA residents, add 6% sales tax). I am enclosing $2.95 plus 75¢ handling fee for *each* book ordered.

Total Amount Enclosed: $＿＿＿＿＿．

＿＿ No. 91	＿＿ No. 96	＿＿ No. 102	＿＿ No. 108
＿＿ No. 159	＿＿ No. 97	＿＿ No. 103	＿＿ No. 109
＿＿ No. 90	＿＿ No. 98	＿＿ No. 104	＿＿ No. 110
＿＿ No. 92	＿＿ No. 99	＿＿ No. 105	＿＿ No. 111
＿＿ No. 93	＿＿ No. 100	＿＿ No. 106	＿＿ No. 112
＿＿ No. 94	＿＿ No. 101	＿＿ No. 107	＿＿ No. 113

Please Print:
Name ＿＿＿＿＿＿＿＿＿＿＿＿＿＿＿＿＿＿＿＿＿＿＿＿＿＿＿＿＿＿＿＿
Address ＿＿＿＿＿＿＿＿＿＿＿＿＿＿＿＿＿＿＿ Apt. No. ＿＿＿＿＿
City/State ＿＿＿＿＿＿＿＿＿＿＿＿＿＿＿＿＿＿＿ Zip ＿＿＿＿＿＿

Allow four to six weeks for delivery. Quantities limited.